Ghost In The Capitol

Illustrations by Gay Haff Kovach

GHOST IN THE CAPITOL

by Idella Bodie

SANDLAPPER
PUBLISHING, INC.

GHOST IN THE CAPITOL

Sixth printing, 2002

Published by Sandlapper Publishing Co., Inc.
Orangeburg, South Carolina 29115

MANUFACTURED IN THE UNITED STATES OF AMERICA

Library of Congress Cataloging-in-Publication Data

Bodie, Idella.
        Ghost in the capitol.

        Summary: Three youngsters are determined to meet
the poltergeist which seems to inhabit the State Capitol
in Columbia, South Carolina.
        1. Ghosts—Fiction.   2. South Carolina—Fiction
I. Kovach, Gay Haff, ill.   II. Title.
PZ7.B63525Gh   1986   [Fic]   86-6702
ISBN 0-87844-072-0 (pbk.)

To my young readers

OTHER BOOKS BY IDELLA BODIE

Contents

Ghost In The Capitol

I.

Ghost in the Capitol

Jill Johnston had finished her science homework, and now she squirmed restlessly in her back row desk. Working her fingers into the watch pocket of her worn jeans, she pulled up her Big Ben with its comforting tick. A half hour to go.

She scooted down in her desk and sighed. Leaning over, she put one clinched fist on top of the other and rested her chin in the niche. Her short potato-colored hair fell forward. Outside, birds chattered in the budding courtyard.

She became lost in thought. Why did Steve's father have to go and get transferred all the way to Washington? He'd probably never even come back to South Carolina.

Papers rustled, somebody coughed, and someone else sharpened a pencil. If Miss Maynard didn't soon call a halt to science, there wasn't going to be enough time

1

for current events. Jill was anxious for everyone to hear David Peoples's report. It was neat. But then Aunt Becky always found him good ones.

Jill rolled her eyes in David's direction. He was through with his science too, but knowing him, he probably had not answered all the questions. She watched him as he practiced reading his current event clipping, his lips mutely forming each word.

Their families were always telling Jill and David that they'd been together so much they looked alike. In fact, they said, Jill looked more like David than she did her own brothers. Why adults always had to decide who young people looked like, she didn't know. Admittedly, their hair was the same color and length, and they were about the same size, as Jill had already had her spurt of growth and David's was yet to come. But Jill had green eyes—cat eyes her brother Rod called them—and David's eyes were dark brown.

Jill sighed again. What a great trio she, David, and Steve had made! But Steve had moved, and she had to stop dwelling on it. As Aunt Becky always said, "There's no need to cry over spilled milk."

Finally Miss Maynard stood up, her blonde hair bobbing. "All right, class, if you aren't through answering your science questions, finish them up at home."

Books slapped shut. There was a mumble around the room as different ones remarked what number they were on. Only Bernard Thornburg, the new boy from New York, did not look up. He'd been assigned Steve's old desk, but as Jill looked at him now, she couldn't help thinking how different he was from Steve. Already he'd gotten the reputation of being an *Einstein*. As he bent low over the thick book he was reading, the black elastic band holding his thick-lensed glasses in place made his stubby brown hair stick out like a porcupine.

Jill was concentrating so hard on Bernard's appearance that she was afraid she might have missed her chance to ask Miss Maynard to let David go first. Without putting up her hand for permission, she blurted out, "Miss Maynard, let David do his."

"All right, David," replied Miss Maynard as she shot Jill one of her famous disapproving looks for the outburst. Then she lowered her slender frame into a vacant desk at the front of the room.

Jill liked Miss Maynard for a teacher, even if she had moved her across the room from David and did sometimes seem to have it in for her.

David slid out of his desk and made his way to the front of the class. Jill could tell he was having a hard time keeping back a grin. "My report is on 'Is the State Capitol Spooked?'" He looked up to get the reaction of the class and wriggled his feet into a good position.

Every head in the room turned toward David. Even Bernard's shot up and he blurted out, "I saw that!"

Oh, he would! thought Jill.

"Just a moment, Bernard." As always Miss Maynard was polite but firm. "We'll discuss it *after* David has finished his report."

David lifted his chin and shook his head to work his hair back from his face. His voice was loud and clear as he began to read his news clipping.

Another night security officer has resigned his position at the State Capitol. C. D. Harvey refused to give notice, claiming "noises and crazy goings-on around that place" were too much for him.

"Ever since I began noticing the peculiarities," he said,

3

"it's unnerved me so I can't sleep when I get home."

When asked to comment, most employees of the Capitol Building were noncommittal; however, one outspoken clerk remarked that Harvey was the third night security employee this year to leave.

Another security guard just laughed when he was questioned by this reporter. "Oh," he said, "somebody comes up with an old ghost tale about this place every fifty years or so."

But to Nightwatchman Harvey, it's no laughing matter.

Even before David started to his seat, Bernard's arm shot up. A boy in the back yelled, "Say, aren't we supposed to go to the Capitol next week, Miss Maynard?"

Suddenly the class was in an uproar. Jill watched in disgust as some girls hugged themselves, scrunched up in their desks, and let out fakey little twitters. Why did most girls have to act so sissified? she wondered.

"Hot dog!" A tow-headed boy slapped his knee. "Maybe we'll see a ghost."

"Not me," a girl with a thin voice called out. "I don't like ghosts."

"You ought to," somebody piped up, "'cause you're one."

"Class!" Miss Maynard stood.

Bernard was waving his arm like a brakeman in a railroad station yard.

"Just a minute!" Miss Maynard said, her voice now louder.

Jill flashed David a smile across the room and rounded her fingers into an *O*. She'd told him his clipping would be a hit.

"Now," Miss Maynard said when she had finally gotten the class under control, "let's hear Bernard."

Faint moans passed around the room. Bernard's long-winded manner of speaking hadn't won him any friends. He seemed so different from the rest of the class. He always had his nose in a book. And he dressed funny. He didn't wear jeans to school like everybody else, but white shirts and pants pulled in with a belt around his high waist.

Now as Bernard twisted in his desk and tilted his head in preparation to speak, Jill caught the full expression of his face. It gave absolutely no clue to his feelings. Of one thing she felt sure—Bernard didn't have the faintest idea that people thought he was peculiar.

"Yes, Bernard?" asked Miss Maynard. Jill felt she was trying hard to be patient.

Bernard pursed his thin lips and cut at the air with his small, pale arm. Then he began in his monotone, "There are many different kinds of ghosts. From what I've read, it appears that the one referred to in this article is a *poltergeist*."

Giggles gave way to open laughs. Jill stiffened. This poor guy didn't even know everybody was laughing at him.

"Oh?" questioned Miss Maynard, her gaze and voice sympathetic. "And could you tell the class just what kind of *ghost* this is, Bernard?" She acted as if she hated to say the word *ghost*.

"Well, Miss Maynard—" He paused and gestured theatrically. "David's ghost seems to be the *good kind*."

A girl in a purple shirt put both hands up to her mouth and giggled shrilly into them. The room broke into chaos.

"*My* **ghost**?" yelled David.

"If you ask me," the tow-headed boy shouted, "there ain't no such thing as a good ghost!"

Jill straightened up in her desk. She felt happier than

she had at any time since Steve moved away.

"All right!" Miss Maynard rapped her desk with a ruler. "If this is the way you're going to act, perhaps we'd better cancel our tour of the State House."

There was a round of Shhhhhhh's, and then an abnormal silence fell over the room.

"All right," she repeated. This time her voice was lower, but it was evident she was having trouble keeping it that way. "Now let's move along."

"Miss Maynard?"

"Yes, Jill?"

"What really is a *pol–ter*—whatever Bernard said?"

Miss Maynard looked as if she'd rather forget the whole thing, but she sighed and said, "Bernard, would you like to tell the class—briefly—what you were referring to?"

"Yes, Miss Maynard." Bernard pursed his lips, clipping his nasal twang. With a wave of his hand he began. "A poltergeist is a spirit of someone who has returned to haunt a place he once inhabited when he was alive. In some way he, or some form of his memory, is still attached to the scene of a tragedy. He might be coming back to be near another person or to look for some lost possession."

"But if he's a spirit," asked Jill shifting in her desk, "how do you know he's there?"

"Well," Bernard began, his slender fingers cutting across the air as he talked, "he makes himself evident by making noises—mostly raps and knocks. Sometimes poltergeists move objects."

Faces around the room registered shock and downright disbelief.

"Can we hear him when we go to the Capitol?"

6

somebody asked.

"Oh, I don't think so," Bernard went on confidently. "He won't likely manifest himself with lots of people about." He tilted his head back, causing his glasses to catch the light at odd angles and reflect it like a prism. "It is rather unusual though—he's known as a noise ghost, but I don't think he likes noises."

"But why," asked David above the mumbling of the other students, "did you say he was a *good* ghost?"

"Because," said Bernard with utmost seriousness, "these ghosts don't bother people."

"He wouldn't have to bother me," giggled the girl in the purple. "He would scare me to death first."

Everybody laughed. Even Miss Maynard smiled.

The discussion grew livelier. Jill thought Miss Maynard had a resigned look on her face, and before they knew it, the bell rang. For the first time since Jill could remember, there wasn't a mad dash for the door.

Lots of people crowded around Bernard. "How do you know all this?" Jill asked.

"Where we lived in New York, my father taught courses in parapsychology. He's got loads of books on ESP and related fields," he said.

Bernard didn't seem the least bit affected by all the attention. Except for the occasional pursing of his thin lips, his expression didn't change.

"I've seen you on our bus," said David. "Where do you live?"

"Claire Towers."

"Say—" Jill exclaimed, "that's right near David and me. I live in one of those big old two-story houses on Pendleton Street and he's on Marion."

Even as Jill said it, something she couldn't identify

held her back. The mental picture of the day they had played catch with the book Bernard was reading during lunch break edged itself into her mind.

Students were scattering now, and Miss Maynard looked up from straightening her desk. "It sounds as if David's report opened up a whole new world," she said. Jill noticed that her voice was back to normal.

"A spooky one," Jill said.

"Not really," said Bernard

David wanted to know more. "I'd like to see some of those books on that *pol–ter–guy.* Is it all right if me and Jill come by your place?"

Jill laughed. "You read a book, David Peoples? Who're you trying to kid?" Jill's voice was louder than she'd meant it to be, and Miss Maynard shot her another of her looks.

"Well, what do you think I asked Barnard if you could come for? You can read it to me."

"Sure, it's okay," said Bernard. "My dad won't mind."

With a pang of sadness Jill thought of Steve.

II.

Witches and Ghosts

That night when Jill crawled into bed, she thought about how great the day had turned out. Except for the scolding she'd received for getting home late, it had been perfect.

After school, David had suggested they go straight to Bernard's apartment at Claire Towers. That suited Jill—because once she got home, she'd never be able to get away from her pesky brothers.

Inside the Thornburgs' fifth-floor apartment, Jill and David couldn't believe their eyes. Neither of them had ever seen so many books except in a library. The built-in bookcases were overflowing, and more shelves made of stacked bricks and boards covered every wall but one. On that wall was a worn-looking couch. Other than that, there were just floor pillows, lamps, and a table with a chess game set up. Nothing was prissy the way most people she knew kept their living rooms.

"Do both your parents work?" Jill asked.

"Yes," said Bernard. "They're professors at the University of South Carolina."

"You an only child?" asked David.

"Yes, I am."

"Me too," David said, "but my parents are divorced, and I live with my grandmother and she keeps boarders."

"You lucky stiffs," groaned Jill.

Bernard looked at her rather curiously.

"Jill's got five brothers," David explained.

'Yeah—gross!" said Jill, reaching for a book. "But I've got a really great cat named Beelzebub."

"Is he black?" asked Bernard.

"Black as soot."

"Which books have ghosts in them?" David asked, as he scanned the shelves.

"Well—" said Bernard, depositing his heavy book satchel on the table, "there's something you need to know first."

Jill and David exchanged glances. Had they come up here for nothing?

"You see," Bernard began, sounding much like a professor himself, "people don't really understand ghosts at all. That's why they dress up on Halloween and run around scaring each other."

This poor guy, thought Jill. *Hasn't he ever had any fun?*

"If people really comprehended ghosts," Bernard went on, his hands in motion, "they'd know that ghosts don't go in for that kind of thing at all."

This was too much. Jill put her hands on her hips and faced him squarely. "Don't tell me, Bernard

10

Thornburg, that you've never been 'trick or treating.'"

"Well—maybe—when I was young. But I surely never pretended I was a ghost."

"I give up." Jill rolled her eyes at David. And in the next breath she said, "Say, there's a book that has witches in it. See—*Witchcraft USA*."

"Now," said Bernard, "that's another matter entirely."

"Don't tell me you don't believe in witches either, Bernard!" Jill cast a knowing look in David's direction. "You know—those black-clad things that ride through the night on broomsticks?"

"No, I don't," said Bernard, completely unaware that Jill was pulling his leg. "At least not the kind of witch you're talking about. There are, however, people with supernatural powers, and long ago these persons were burned at the stake."

"Well, I know that." Jill pursed her mouth in thought. *This guy wouldn't know a joke if it slapped him in the face.* "I've read *Witch of Blackbird Pond*." For once her tone was serious.

"What about *The Scarlet Letter*?" asked Bernard.

"Not me," said Jill dully. "Try David." Out of the corner of her eye she saw David stick out his tongue at her.

"Okay, you two," said David, "I thought we came up here to look up that polter–thingamajig. Grandma'll be hollering for me pretty soon."

"Oh, my gosh," said Jill. "I forgot about calling Mom. Where's your phone, Bernard?"

"We don't have one."

"*You don't have one?*"

"No. My parents think they're a nuisance. There's one in the lobby downstairs."

12

'Yeah, Jill," grinned David, "the quarter kind."

"The word is *poltergeist*," Bernard said, as if he had not heard the telephone discussion. He moved to another bookcase and took down a thick black book entitled *An Explanation of Haunted Houses*.

David and Jill closed in around him as he flipped to the glossary. Bringing it up closer to his thick lenses, he quickly ran his finger down the page until he came to the word poltergeist.

"See," he said, "you pronounce it *pol—ter—geist*."

"Go ahead," urged David. "Read it."

Holding the book close, Bernard began reading aloud. "A ghost or spirit supposed to manifest its presence by noises or knockings. It is thought that a poltergeist occurrence may have something to do with a person living in a house. See pages 111-115."

"Okay, turn there," ordered David impatiently.

"I believe," said Bernard as he flipped backward in the book, that this is the one that gives accounts of some famous poltergeists."

"There," said Jill. "There it is." Putting her hand out to steady the book she began to read aloud. "A special kind of ghost is one called the *pol–ter–gee*—"

"Poltergeist," Bernard prompted.

Ignoring him, Jill read on. "The name comes from a German word that means a noisy ghost. Poltergeists are associated with particular houses or buildings. Sometimes the movements occur in rooms where no people are present. At other times strange happenings take place before family members or friends or investigators. These strange happenings are usually accompanied by footsteps, scrapings, raps, bumps, and knocks. Sometimes objects appear to throw themselves about. People can even be struck by these flying objects."

"Wait a minute," blurted David. "I thought you said he was a good ghost."

"Well," Bernard answered, "I did. Because, you see, he isn't really *after* people. He's either coming back to claim something he's left behind or hanging around one certain person."

"And that person's you, David," hollered Jill. Then she balled up her fist and let David have it on his upper arm.

"Oh, no you don't either," he said, giving her a push. "I didn't find him. Aunt Becky picked out that article, and you know it."

Jill laughed and jabbed her finger at another place in the book. "There's something on spirits—"

"That's *spiritualism*," said Bernard. "That's communicating with the dead, but it's not quite the same thing as we're dealing with." And in the next breath he said, "Here. Here is a poltergeist case that tells about a girl in Scotland whose bed was shaken by a spirit. It moved her pillow. The spirit even followed her to school, and her teacher saw it lift her desk."

"Ah, gimmie that," David demanded. He pulled the book nearer and began to read. "In Virginia's bedroom the knocks continued at night. Strange rotation of the bed and pillow were observed. Two physicians brought a tape recorder and camera into the room, but they were never able to get the camera going quickly enough to capture the movements. The recorder did pick up the sounds of a sawing or rasping noise."

A shiver ran over Jill. "Hey," she said, "it's gloomy in here. Where's the light switch?"

Bernard reached behind him and switched on the

14

overhead light while David turned the page, only to find the beginning of another tale. "You mean that's all there is about Virginia?" he asked.

"Most of these cases are unsolved," said Bernard. "That's why they're called ghost stories."

By now Jill and David were so accustomed to Bernard's manner of waving his hands about when he spoke they hardly noticed it as he went on. "Some of the ghosts, however, do get exorcised—especially poltergeists."

"*Exorcised?*" asked Jill.

"Yes. If these *spirits* find what they're looking for, they'll leave."

"Really?" she mused. "You mean if David's ghost can find what he's looking for, then he'll leave?"

"It's not quite so simple," said Bernard. "There's a lot more to it."

"And, Jill Johnston," said David, "if you don't stop calling him *my* ghost, there's going to be a **heck** of a lot more—like a busted head!"

"Actually," Bernard said laboriously, "this kind of spirit has to have a person to take power from. So in a way, David, he is your ghost."

"What about the guards who quit their jobs?" asked David indignantly. "Maybe he was taking power from them."

"Well, that's right," said Bernard. "Somebody has to activate the spirit each time he makes himself evident. On the other hand, it is believed that poltergeists prefer young people about our age."

"Oooooh," said Jill with a nervous giggle, "that next one is called 'Bottle Popping Mystery.' That doesn't sound very spooky."

15

"Oh," said Bernard, "there's an excellent account of that in my father's *Journal of Parapsychology*. It's rather long though. It happened in a house where a boy and girl who were twelve and thirteen lived. The parents thought one of the children was breaking all the bottles or somebody else was doing it for pranks. They had the police in and had all kinds of engineers check the house for unusual frequencies."

"You mean everything in bottles was popped?" asked David.

"Yes—or spilled—shampoo, cologne, and even kaopectate for upset stomachs." For a moment Jill thought she saw a trace of a smile on Bernard's face.

"So what happened?" David asked eagerly.

"Nothing," replied Bernard. "Like most of them, the case was never solved. As I said, that's why they're called ghost stories."

"Then *our* ghost," said Jill, "and do take notice, David, I said *our* ghost, may just stop of his own accord."

"Oh, I doubt it—not if he's looking for some possession—not until he finds it. Now he may stay dormant for awhile, but he'll come back."

They read greedily on and the afternoon flew by. Jill found it hard to believe that David could be so interested in reading. He kept pulling books from the shelf and saying, "Listen to this."

Later, as Jill lay in her front upstairs bedroom, the street light made familiar patterns on her walls. She thought over all they had read, weighing and sifting it in her mind. Much of what they heard she didn't understand—all about how physicists and mathematicians are now aware that space has dimensions and that

16

houses and furniture may hold memories of earlier happenings. But then, Jill supposed, if it could be understood it wouldn't be mysterious.

A scratch on the screen startled Jill. Then she realized it was Beelzebub. He always came up by way of the wisteria vine and the gabled roof when he was locked out downstairs.

Jill leaned over and pushed out the loose corner of the screen. By the light from the street lamp she watched him nudge into the opening and wind his body through. Like a dark shadow he pounced onto Jill's bed.

Beelzebub moved restlessly as Jill reached to tuck the screen back into place. "Mosquitoes, you are not welcome," she said. For some reason Jill felt it was all right to talk to herself when Beelzebub was around. It was really like having another person there.

Jill put her hand down to stroke the soft black fur as Beelzebub turned round and round until he found just the right spot against Jill's legs. The warmth of his body was comforting.

"Beelzebub," she said, fingering his velvet ears, "you old night cat—where have you been?"

Beelzebub purred.

Jill's mind turned quickly back to the events of the afternoon. There was another thing that puzzled her: she didn't see how an individual's consciousness could separate itself from his body. Could the soul of the dead really leave the body and travel? Does the soul not go to its resting place immediately but stay around to haunt a place? This must be what happened in the case of the polter–thingamajig.

Jill didn't feel sleepy. She bunched her pillow so she could look out of the tall window by her bed, although there was never much to see at the other houses. Most of their neighbors were older people, and they went to bed early. Once, though, Jill had seen a patrol car chasing a speeding motorist up their street.

Somewhere in the house a chair scraped and something bumped interrupting Jill's thoughts. She snuggled beneath her light covers. It was *never* quiet in their house with all those boys. Why should she expect it to be different tonight? She wondered if the younger boys had come up to bed. They always stayed up later on Friday nights, but usually Mom made them stagger their bed times so Michael wouldn't pick on Jeff. Rod and Larry, the two older boys, had separate bedrooms, but they regularly stayed up late—except that Rod sometimes read in bed. Jill, being the only girl, had a room all to herself. That was what she liked best about their house—there were six bedrooms. Mom liked to keep Bobby, who was two and a half, downstairs near her.

Jill suddenly felt glad she had an upstairs bedroom. At least nobody could be hanging around her windows. Then she remembered, *they weren't dealing with people but with spirits.* Jill closed her eyes tightly and wrapped her knees around Beelzebub's warm, soft body. She didn't want to watch the shadows play over her room tonight.

Would she dream? she wondered. Would her subconscious, which had remained buried in the back of her mind, become active during sleep?

Where, she wondered, *would all this lead?*

III.

Aunt Becky

Jill woke early for a Saturday. Before she drifted off to sleep the night before, she had decided that she and David would take Bernard to meet Aunt Becky.

Everyone called her Aunt Becky although she wasn't really anyone's aunt. She had always lived in the boardinghouse David's grandmother kept, and everybody called her that—including the university students who stayed there. With Bernard's knowledge of spirits and Aunt Becky's of old Columbia, the two of them would be great together.

Jill eased Beelzebub's relaxed body over and watched him arch his back and stretch out, spreading his claws. In a sunlight too young to cast a shadow, Jill slipped out of bed, pulled on her jeans and T-shirt, and dabbed a brush at her short brown hair. With a disapproving glance at hair that couldn't decide which way to curve, she started downstairs.

19

On her way past her older brothers' rooms, Jill saw that they were still asleep. Downstairs, she found her younger brothers already up. The middle brother Michael had the two younger boys seated at the table. "I'm getting our breakfast," he announced, "and letting Mom sleep."

"That's good," said Jill. "But, hey, Jeff, go easy on that milk. Your cereal's swimming." And in the next breath, "And what, Bobby Johnston, are you doing with my gym shoes on?"

"I don't know," he said as he looked down at the flopping canvas shoes on his feet and primped to cry.

"Okay. Okay," said Jill in despair. Knowing he would not only wake Mom but alarm the whole neighborhood, she added, "Wear them, but for pity sakes, come here and let me tie up the laces so you'll stop walking on them."

Jill grabbed a sweet roll from the bread box. Pushing open the screened door, she yelled over her shoulder, "Tell Mom I'm at David's." She headed across the back lot to the two-storied yellow boardinghouse on Marion Street.

Dew showered her as she wriggled through their special pass through the shrubbery. There was something Jill liked about early mornings, *especially Saturdays*. The air smelled fresh and clean.

David's grandmother was bustling around the kitchen as usual. Her maid didn't come on weekends since most of the college boys went home. Her pretty gray hair was piled on top of her head in fluffy curls and already her face was slightly flushed from hurrying about. "Oh, hi, Jill. Come on in. I don't think old sleepyhead David is up yet."

"Oh, yes he is," said David, craning his neck around the hall entry.

"Come along then," said his grandmother, "and stick this toast in for me. Aunt Becky hasn't been served yet."

David's right, thought Jill. *Every time he comes close to his grandmother, she thinks of something for him to do.* In a way it was like her mom's nagging her about picking up after herself. She figured you just had to learn to live with it.

"Do you think it would be all right," asked Jill, "if we brought the new boy over to meet Aunt Becky this morning?"

"Oh, I'm sure Aunt Becky would enjoy that," she answered as she leaned to peek in the oven. "What about some toast for you, Jill?"

"Oh, no thank you. I'll mosey on over and get Bernard and then come back." As an afterthought she added, "His family doesn't have a phone."

There was no one stirring on Marion Street as Jill headed toward Claire Towers. As she walked she thought of Aunt Becky. Long ago David told her that when his grandmother decided to keep only college boys, she felt Aunt Becky was too much like part of the family to ask her to move. Ever since, the life of the boardinghouse seemed to center around this perky little old lady who sat by her window in a wheel chair and read through a magnifying glass.

Even though the business-like clerk in the lobby of Claire Towers smiled at Jill, she felt a little odd about going up to Bernard's apartment. The halls were dim and when there was no answer to her knock, Jill was beginning to wish she hadn't come.

Once again in the lobby, Jill cringed as the clerk

said, "Could I help you, *little lady?*"

"I was looking for Bernard Thornburg."

"Oh, you'll find him in the museum on Sumter Street if it's open or on the State House grounds."

Outside once again in the yellow morning sunlight, Jill turned onto Senate Street and started toward the Capitol. All the offices in the government buildings were closed on Saturdays so traffic was light in the city.

It was going to be great, Jill thought, when they got Aunt Becky and Bernard together. For as many years as she could remember she'd loved hearing Aunt Becky's stories of old Columbia, but this time would be different. Now they would be listening for something special—very special. They would be listening for a clue—a clue to why a ghost might be haunting the Capitol. Jill's heart raced just thinking about it, and she quickened her pace.

Before she got to the State House grounds with its tall oaks and magnolias, she glimpsed the white shirt of a seated figure. There was Bernard, sitting on a bench by a statue, his body bent low over a book.

Until Jill reached him and called his name, he was unaware of her presence. Even then, he came up from his book reluctantly.

When Bernard and Jill arrived at David's, his grandmother had him taking out the garbage, so they went on in the house. Aunt Becky's room was filled with the perfumed smell of artificial flowers and talcum powder. She was pouring steaming tea, somewhat shakily, from her little teapot.

Jill noticed that her red lipstick and eyebrows had already been painted on. It had always fascinated Jill that Aunt Becky drew brownish-red lines from somewhere up on her forehead down past the corners of her eyes, fixing her face with a permanent *surprised* look.

As soon as Aunt Becky spotted them from across the heavily draped room, she flashed a broad, false-toothy grin, wrinkling her rough cheeks.

"Come in. Come in." The little muscular twitch on the left side of her mouth set itself to work, and she lifted an arthritic hand to pat her yellow fuzz of hair in place for her guests.

"Aunt Becky," Jill said, "this is Bernard. He has a photogenic mind."

"Ah." Aunt Becky's eyebrows came together at the center. "Is that a fact, young man?"

"Well, no it isn't," said Bernard, not the least bit bothered by the way Jill had introduced him. "I believe Jill meant *photographic* mind, but I really don't have one hundred percent total recall—not by test and measurement standards. But I do like to read, and I remember almost all of what I read."

"Um–hump," responded Aunt Becky, "and I see you have a book there now." She dipped a spoonful of tea from her cup and blew on it. A wisp of steam whirled upward as she sipped, making little sucking noises with her thin red lips.

At that moment David walked into the room, and the three of them sat on the floral carpet at Aunt Becky's feet. Jill's mind quickly flooded with memories. How many times she, David, and Steve had sat there listening to Aunt Becky's stories!

"Aunt Becky," asked David, as eager as Jill to get on with things, "do you believe in the supernatural?"

"Well, now, David, that's a big question." Her voice sounded mysterious, much as it did when she told ghost stories.

"Well," asked Jill, "do you believe a person's conscious can separate itself from the body and exist after death?"

"I've heard tales of such," Aunt Becky confirmed. Then, she leaned over, and lowering her voice said, "In the coastal part of South Carolina, there was a woman who dreamed she was walking around rooms in an old country house. Later on, her husband took her there on vacation. The owner of the old house was shocked when he saw her. Then he explained to her that she had been there before *as a ghost*."

Suddenly Jill knew why stories in this room had always intrigued her so. The darkly draped room with its powdery fragrance and Aunt Becky's voice fluctuating just at the right places—all of it, even the little twitch in Aunt Becky's face that seemed to come at just the right moment, held her spellbound.

"Yes, sirree, bobtail squirrel ginny," Aunt Becky said with an odd little laugh. "And the singular thing was the woman had described the house to her husband in telling her dream—even before she had ever seen it."

"Grandma doesn't believe in such things," said David. "I asked her this morning. She says superstition is a sign of ignorance."

"Well—" Aunt Becky's expression showed she didn't want to go against David's grandmother. "I'll tell you something—" Again her voice lowered to almost a whisper. "When your grandma was a little girl, her mother and I took her to get a wart talked off her hand. That old man tied a string around her finger and said some nonsense words, and your great-grandma came home and buried that string right out there by that very kitchen door."

"Gol—ly," marveled David. "Why don't I do that with mine?" He rubbed the warts on the back of his right hand.

"Oh, I don't know as you could find anyone who would do it nowadays." Aunt Becky rubbed at the knobs on the joints of her own drawn hands. "Anyway, there's no need to tell your grandma I told you. She's a good soul, and everybody's entitled to his own beliefs."

"Bernard's got books on ghosts," said Jill, "and there's a special one on *pol–ter–geists*." Jill still pronounced the word falteringly. "Tell her about it, Bernard."

"All right." Bernard removed his hands from his knees to get them ready for action. "A poltergeist is a spirit that has returned to a particular place to look for someone or some possession he lost there when he was a real person."

"Oh, yes," said Aunt Becky, "I know what you mean—I just hadn't heard him called by that name."

Jill couldn't restrain herself any longer.

"And we think, Aunt Becky, that the ghost in the Capitol Building might be that kind—the kind that's come back to look for something."

"O–o–oh," Aunt Becky exclaimed. "Now I know what brought all this on! It was that current event I got for you, wasn't it, Davie?" She slapped her knobby hands on her lap in excitement.

"And what we want to know," said David, "is who he is and what he's doing there."

"Well, well." Aunt Becky shook her head. "This is something else!"

"Will you help us?" David asked.

25

"Now, now, David, telling stories about ghosts and witches is one thing, but getting on familiar terms with them is something else again. . . . And your grandmother—"

"But you said not to mention it, and that everyone was entitled to his own opinion," he pointed out.

"Yes." She spoke thoughtfully, and Jill noticed that her eyebrows were almost horizontal. "That I did—"

Jill looked at Bernard and for the first time she noticed the title of the book he was reading when she found him on the Capitol grounds. "Say, Bernard's got a book on *Sherman's March Through the Carolinas.* Maybe it had something to do with that."

"Aw, that was two hundred years ago," scorned David.

"Oh, no," Bernard corrected, "the Civil War was fought in 1865. That wasn't much over a hundred years ago. But anyway, with poltergeists, time doesn't matter."

"I guess I was thinking of the Revolutionary War. I always get them mixed up."

"You would, dummy," teased Jill.

"Oh, that's easy to do," Aunt Becky explained, "especially for South Carolinians, because battles in both wars were fought in this state. But of course the Revolutionary War was fought between the Colonies and our mother country England, whereas the Civil War was between the North and South in our own country."

"Over owning slaves," said Jill, eager to get her two cents in.

"The first shot in the Civil War was fired on Fort Sumter by the Citadel cadets in Charleston," offered Bernard. "They fired upon a Federal supply ship named *The Star of the West.*"

26

"Don't *know-it-all*s make you sick?"

Accustomed to Jill's manner of speaking, Aunt Becky waved her hand in a "hush now" manner and said, "And what a sad thing that began—brother against brother. Many's the time I heard my grandmother tell the tragic happenings during the burning of Columbia."

"Do you mean your grandmother was here then?" asked Bernard. Jill thought she detected a change in his expression.

"She was just a young girl—newly married—and her husband was off fighting in Tennessee." Aunt Becky was momentarily lost in thought. "Oh, yes, my grandmother remembered it same as yesterday till her dying day."

Nobody said anything, and Aunt Becky went on. "As a matter of fact, all the men were on the battlefield, from the Potomac to the Mississippi—except, that is, the very young and the very old. No indeed, those left behind were no match for the Federal troops."

"It was all Sherman's fault," said David.

"I think you have to consider all the circumstances before you can say that about General William Tecumseh Sherman," argued Bernard.

"After all," Jill retorted, "Bernard's *a damn Yankee*."

"Oh, we don't hold to that today, dearie," Aunt Becky hurried to say.

"Aw, I know that, Aunt Becky. I'm just trying to teach Bernard to take a joke." Jill laughed.

"Well, now," continued Aunt Becky, "we do have to remember that both sides acted under duty and devotion."

"But Sherman didn't have to burn Columbia," David said critically. "The city had surrendered, hadn't

27

it?"

"That's a war tactic," replied Bernard in his matter-of-fact tone. "It always has been."

"Let's have another Civil War," mocked Jill, getting up on her haunches.

"Now, now," soothed Aunt Becky. "It's understandable that Sherman would destroy arsenals, machine shops, and the like—Bernard is right about that. They are legitimate targets of warfare. But he has never been forgiven for the destruction of private homes."

"See, Bernard," jeered Jill, settling down again.

"Why, my grandmother," Aunt Becky went on sadly, "said Sherman's men spoiled food they couldn't carry away, leaving women and children destitute. They even slaughtered horses and left their carcasses to rot on the spot."

"But South Carolina was the first to secede from the Union," defended Bernard, "and the soldiers were angry with her."

"True," Aunt Becky admitted, "but you should have heard my grandmother tell about what a fine old city Columbia was with its tailor shops, daguerreotype studios—that's for making pictures—and its printing offices."

"Did she ever see Sherman?" asked Jill.

"No, she never saw him, but she knew folk that did. They say he was a red-haired, tall, disheveled fellow who, believe it or not, did have a heart. He spared a building in Columbia because a Sister sent him a note asking protection for her convent. He also sent her word that there would be no destruction of private property."

"But there was," quibbled David.

"It could have been that some of his men disobeyed

orders," Aunt Becky explained. "Nevertheless, when the war was over, many of his own people in the North turned against him because they thought he was far too generous with the South in his peace terms."

Caught up in the burning of Columbia and momentarily forgetting about their ghost, Jill asked, "Where was your grandmother that night, Aunt Becky?"

"Much of the night she was in a cemetery." Aunt Becky laced her gnarled fingers together and shook her head sadly. "Their home pillaged and plundered and her wedding ring stripped off her finger, she huddled with others seeking relief from the February chill and the heat of the fire."

"But didn't some people leave the city?" asked Bernard.

"Those who could find room on wagons and trains, but everything was in such a panic that night with burning scraps of cotton lifting in the air." Aunt Becky closed her eyes and the thin skin wrinkled over them.

"But," questioned David, "if nobody got killed, how could my—*our*—ghost be connected with that?"

"Oh, there were some who got killed," acknowledged Aunt Becky, livening up again. "I don't know that you'll find it recorded in history, but there were rumors that some of the Union soldiers died of their own doing. Some had burning buildings collapse on them; others were in a drunken stupor from the Southerners' wine cellars."

"Anyway," said Bernard, "it wouldn't be necessary for our spirit to be killed on that particular spot to be looking for some possession there."

"That's right," Aunt Becky agreed. "Sometimes these *spirits*, as Bernard calls them, just attach themselves to a person they like." She put her hand to her mouth quickly as if she hadn't meant to get involved in this thing.

"Do you know any stories about the State House, Aunt Becky?" Jill asked.

"Oh, you know the main Capitol Building—the one then in use—was destroyed, burned to the ground. Now, there was, come to think of it, a sad tale that had to do with the Capitol we use now—although it was under construction when Sherman marched through."

"Tell it," begged David.

"There was a girl—a doctor's daughter," Aunt Becky began in her best storytelling voice. "A beautiful Southern belle she was. Now it seems that her father, being a doctor, was forced to set the broken leg of a Union soldier. He'd broken it while building another bridge to cross the river into Columbia. You see, our own men had burned the original bridge to slow up the Union soldiers."

Jill thought Aunt Becky looked apologetically at Bernard before she went on. "Now it seems this doctor's daughter—Anna Louisa was her name—had taken care of the soldier until he was able to be moved, and she had fallen in love with him and he with her. When they were forced to part, she gave him her most treasured daguerreotype and a lock of her golden hair. He promised to keep them with him always, until they were reunited forever."

"What did her parents think of it?" asked Jill.

"Oh, they didn't know a thing about it until the night of the burning of Columbia and her parents were ready to flee the city. Anna Louisa refused to go with them and ran through the burning city calling her lover's name."

"Did she find him?" David asked quietly.

"That no one ever knew, but some who stayed behind said they found each other and hid in the Capitol that was then under construction. For many nights thereafter there was a lone light in the Capitol even though no one should have been there, since construction had been discontinued."

"Do you think it was this couple?" questioned Bernard.

"Who knows? . . ." Aunt Becky sighed and closed her eyes. When she opened them, she brought her eyebrows up in their usual perky slant. "My grandmother believed her parents forced her to go; others say she joined the refugees that attached themselves to Sherman's army as it moved north."

For a moment they were all silent. Then Bernard flung his hand up with great vigor. "This could indeed have something to do with David's ghost," he said. "He could be haunting the last place where they were together."

"Young man!" Aunt Becky reached over and put her hand on Bernard's shoulder. "Jill is right—you are a brain."

David's mouth was slightly ajar as if to speak when Jill said, "I was thinking the same thing only Bernard beat me to it."

They all laughed.

"Do you really think the ghost in the Capitol could be that Union soldier searching for his girl?" David asked of no one in particular.

"**Da—vid!**" His grandmother's voice from an upstairs bedroom broke the spell. "I could use some help

31

up here."

As they got up to leave, Jill glared at Bernard. "I still think the Yankees were terrible."

Aunt Becky caught her hand. "You know, Jill," she said, "I used to think so too when I was your age, but now I know that the Yankees, as you call them, and the Rebels were all human beings fighting for causes they believed in. It was many years later I learned there was a prisoner of war camp on the west bank of the Congaree River that treated the Union soldiers mighty bad. In fact, they nicknamed it 'Camp Sorghum' because the men lived mostly on molasses."

As they said goodbye to Aunt Becky, Jill was glad Bernard was not the type to say, "I told you so."

"Come on, Bernard," she said. "Let's go help David and then go to the Capitol grounds."

IV.

The Grounds

The sun was still high when the trio started for the Capitol grounds.

They had helped David sweep the last of the curled brown leaves from the roof by leaning from the gabled windows, and afterward had been treated to sugar cookies and Kool-Aid.

With a warning from David's grandmother not to be gone too long, they made a detour by Jill's house. Michael and Jeff were hammering away at their tree fort in the prongs of the big-rooted oak. Inside the house, Mrs. Johnston was getting ready to go grocery shopping, and Jill was afraid for awhile she would have to keep Bobby.

Even now as they headed toward the State House grounds, she felt a little guilty about it. If she had told Bobby he could feed the pigeons at the Capitol, he'd have wanted to be with her. But she hadn't, and he had whined to go with their mom and got his way. Oh, well, Jill mused, she'd make it up to Mom. This trip was a special one, and having Bobby along could really foul things up.

"You know," said Bernard as they paused for the traffic light at the corner of Marion and Senate Streets, "South Carolina is a very famous state."

"Of course," agreed Jill, resuming her usual good spirits, "David and I were born here."

"Then," Bernard continued, "you know that South Carolina was one of the thirteen original colonies and that King Charles II of England rewarded some friends by making them Lord Proprietors of South Carolina in 1663. By 1670 settlers had established a colony and called it Albemarle Point, but it was soon named in honor of the King and called Charles Town."

Jill stopped dead in her tracks and faced Bernard. "Would you just turn off that sound track, Bernard? What do you say we discuss *only* the history of our state that has something to do with our *polter–guy*? I sure as heck can't remember all this stuff you're forever spouting off, and I don't think David can either."

"Yeah, Bernard. Jill's right. The main thing we gotta do is study the layout of the Capitol and make our plans to get inside the building when the workers aren't there."

"All right," said Bernard as they headed up Senate Street, "but I think you ought to know that South Carolina has provided the nation with one President, Andrew Jackson, and a vice president, John C. Calhoun."

Jill looked at David and threw up her hands. "It's too bad we can't do without this walking encyclopedia," she said. "But, I guess we'll need him before we get this spirit *exorcised* or whatever it is we're going to do

34

to him."

Like a magnet Jill's gaze met David's. This was the first time any one of them had actually put it into words. Even though they had talked all around the subject of sneaking into the Capitol, Jill was sure that David and Bernard had thought of it constantly as she had. They had each known subconsciously what they would try to do.

All in a moment Jill knew why she had not come right out and said it before. She felt jittery when she let herself think about actually trying to get inside the State House and ridding it of the ghost.

Without a doubt, they would need Bernard and his knowledge of such things. Maybe she had hurt his feelings. She certainly couldn't tell by looking at him, for his expression was always the same. Anyway, she hadn't meant to.

"Bernard," she pleaded, "don't get me wrong. We really are glad you're interested in the history of South Carolina. I think that's great, really great, with you just moving here and all, but—"

"As a matter of fact," Bernard replied, and Jill thought his usual monotone brightened somewhat, "I was surprised to learn that there were one hundred and thirty-seven battles fought in South Carolina during the Revolutionary War."

"*Real—ly?*" asked Jill with absolutely no enthusiasm.

They crossed the horseshoe turn on Senate Street in silence and headed toward the spacious State House grounds. Living so close to the Capitol, Jill supposed she had always taken it somewhat for granted. But she had liked coming to the grounds for as long as she could remember. When she was tiny, her father or her older brother Larry would bring her to feed the pigeons.

When they reached the bench where she'd found Bernard reading earlier in the day, Jill plopped down. She just didn't know how to handle Bernard. If you were nice to him, he'd go reeling off those facts again. *Golly,* she thought, *his head must be crammed full.*

David broke the silence. "I'll bet you know all about the people this statue is in honor of, don't you, Bernard?"

"Well, this one," he answered, "is in honor of South Carolina generals and Patriot Sons from 1775 to 1783— chiefly Sumter, Marion, and Pickens. There are some things about them in the museum on Sumter Street, and their portraits hang in the Capitol.

"I absolutely don't understand you, David Peoples!" Jill blurted angrily. "First you say we won't talk about any history that we don't need. And now you egg Bernard on. Why do you think we came over here if it wasn't to make our plans?"

In her anger, she whipped around toward Sumter Street. Traffic was heavy now and the noise from the passing cars and scattered pedestrians were an irritation to her.

"You oughta know, Jill," said David, "that the Capitol isn't open to visitors on Saturdays."

"Of course I know that," said Jill turning again to face the two boys. "But what we need to do today is get the layout of the grounds fixed in our minds. It sure is going to look different at night."

"I don't think that'll be any problem," David remarked. "The front and back are simple with all those steps, and we know George Washington with his broken cane is on the front."

"And," said Jill somewhat sarcastically, "we know his cane was brickbatted by the Union soldiers during the Civil War." She glared at Bernard, and then for some reason she was sorry she had said it. It made her feel the way she did toward Michael when Mom punished him for picking on the younger boys. After all, Bernard couldn't help it that his ancestors were on the other side during the war.

David ignored her and went on. "And Wade Hampton is riding his horse on the backside. Anyway, you couldn't miss knowing which way Main Street is."

"David is right," agreed Bernard. "Our chief concern should be how we're going to get past those security guards and get inside and up into the dome."

A shiver ran up Jill's spine. She had felt Bernard must be thinking along the same lines as she and David, but somehow his saying it made it all the more final.

Jill glanced around to see people milling over the well-kept lawn. Some were talking; others were eating peanuts and feeding the pigeons. A few students were lying on the grass studying, and a family was taking group pictures up near the front steps. Then she saw the uniformed guard walking his post. He had a gun belted to his side, and he slapped a billy stick in rhythm against his right leg as he moved.

Maybe Jill wanted subconsciously to put off thinking about entering the Capitol. She didn't know, but she heard herself say, "We can worry about the inside the day our class comes on tour. I still say we need to familiarize ourselves with the location of all the statues, even the ones on the corners. We might want to use them for code words or signals." She pulled out paper and pen from her pocket. "I got this when we went by my house. Now without looking too obvious, let's just move around and write down locations of the statues and good hiding places in case we have to dart somewhere in a hurry."

"Oh, I don't think we'll need to write anything down," said Bernard.

"Maybe you don't, Bernard, but we do," Jill said, revealing her annoyance.

"I don't think we need to write anything down either," remarked David. "Let's just study it."

"Don't tell me Bernard's photogenic mind is rubbing off on you, David Peoples!"

"It's *photographic*, Jill," corrected Bernard. "But as I said—"

"Well, I don't give a hoot what either one of you say. I'm writing it down."

"Nobody plans to run but you anyway, Jill," said David jovially.

"Me?" Jill was in no mood for jokes.

"Yeah—remember the night you ran out of the Episcopal cemetery without even telling me you were leaving?"

"I told you Steve and I were running from that drunk at the bus stop—not from 'hants' in the graveyard."

"Sure, Jill. Sure," he teased.

"Incidentally," said Bernard, "the South Carolina battles of Kings Mountain and Cowpens were the turning point of the Revolutionary War."

Jill looked at David. She couldn't believe what was taking place. He was actually interested in all this stuff Bernard was spouting off. He wasn't paying her one bit of attention. Right before her eyes he started reading the

39

inscription about the Patriot Sons.

Jill jumped up. She knew she ought to do like her dad always said and count to ten before she said anything, but she didn't care.

"Well, you two just go ahead and cram your silly heads with all that junk we don't need, and I'll do the groundwork." With that she stalked off in the direction of the huge granite State House.

"Come to think of it, Jill," David called after her, "you'd have made a good South Carolinian back then even if you are a girl. They were called Rebels."

Suddenly Jill was boiling mad. *They just couldn't stand for a girl to make the plans. Well, they might as well get used to the idea because times had changed.*

Jill felt herself steaming as she headed around the front of the Capitol Building. She and David had had plenty of spats, but this was the limit. Of all things, he was siding with Bernard Thornburg against her. As she passed George Washington with his broken cane, she was glad she had said what she did.

But the truth of it was David made her so all-fired mad when he acted like her being a girl was the root of all their troubles. *Dad blast it, she was mad.*

Jill stamped right by the cast-iron palmetto tree she usually stopped to admire and down to the west side of the Capitol. Thank goodness there was hardly anyone on the lower side. She needed privacy. Plopping herself onto a bench, she pulled out the pencil and paper she had angrily stuffed into her pocket moments before. Let them run haywire the night of the entry. She wasn't going to help them.

She smoothed out her paper on the seat beside her and began to sketch. First she drew a rectangle in the

center for the Capitol. As an afterthought, she arched in the dome.

"Get inside and up into the dome," Bernard had said. The shiver Jill felt earlier now crept its way up her spine. Everybody knew that ghosts liked attics or the unused parts of buildings and houses. . . . Maybe in this case it was because the dome was nearer the sky and ghosts liked that because they were airborne and favored high places? . . . Jill shook her shoulders to throw off the creepy feeling. She looked up at the great dome with its arched windows. *What is it like up there?* she wondered.

Jill's attention was drawn to a Carolina wren on the grass nearby. She could identify it by its small proportions, its brownish-red feathers, and the white stripe over its eyes. Suddenly it lifted its head and sang, "Tea–ket–tle, tea–ket–tle."

Somehow the little bird softened her anger, and she wished David and Bernard could see it. But of course Bernard would have to give some long spiel about its scientific name and family and all that poppy rot.

A Mack truck revved its motor as it moved along the street, and the little wren perked up its black-barred tail and flew away.

Returning to her sketch, Jill drew in the statues, the man-made palmetto, and some of the larger magnolias. Then she drew in the concrete walks. *Who knows?* she thought. *We might have to head down this way if we get caught, and it could be dangerous running over unfamiliar lawns at night.*

Jill was so absorbed by her sketching she didn't see the security officer until he was almost upon her. As she looked up, he suddenly sidetracked and went another di-

42

rection to break up a couple of teenaged sweethearts.

As the guard started back up the slight incline toward where Jill sat, he noticed her watching him and smiled. "I'm sure," he said, coming closer, "that I would never have to speak to you about such conduct."

"Heck no!" said Jill, her old anger returning. "Boys make me sick."

"Oh, is that so?"

"Yes. I had two friends—both boys—until just a little while ago."

"Had a fight, did you?"

"Yes—" she began, then quickly caught herself. This was the last person she could ever tell about the reason for the fight. The security guards would be the very ones they'd have to outfox the night of the entry. So, instead, she said, "To top it off, I've got five brothers and no sisters."

"Gee!" he exclaimed sympathetically. "You do have it rough." He sat down on the other end of the bench in a way that made Jill think he wouldn't stay long.

Suddenly Jill was aware of her sketch. She folded the image toward the inside. If she tried to hide the entire paper, she thought, he might get suspicious.

"Tell me," she asked, "is anyone ever allowed in the Capitol dome?"

"Nobody but the maintenance men and the man who puts up the flag." They both looked up at the dome as he added, "It's very dangerous up there with the ladder stairs and the catwalks."

"Oh, it has catwalks?" she asked, trying hard not to act too interested.

"Yes, it does. They're used by maintenance men to replace lights and make repairs. They do have rails, but it's far too dangerous for use by the general public." He rose from the bench and survey the grounds. "There's really not much to see up there."

"Do you work at night?" Jill asked as he turned to go.

"No, I don't. I don't believe they could get me to do that."

"Why not?" she asked eagerly. *Had she hit upon something they could use?*

Her hopes fell as he said, "Oh, I don't think I could do much sleeping in the daytime." Continuing to look all about him, he said, "Well, I'll be seeing you."

Jill managed a smile. Shucks! she thought. If only he hadn't been in such a hurry, maybe she could have worked their conversation around to some information that might have helped.

"Take it easy," he said over his shoulder. "All of us men aren't so bad."

Jill realized it was time to go home. She was still put out with David and Bernard, so she decided she would leave by the back way. Let them wonder what had happened to her. She didn't give a hoot.

Following the curving walkways, she went around the back of the building, past Wade Hampton sitting astride his great horse. She had a sudden urge to pet the great stallion, and tiptoeing she rubbed his flank. Jill smiled as she remembered the day long ago when she and her dad had found Michael sitting on the horse behind General Hampton. Michael was such a monkey.

As Jill left the area where she'd been hidden from the boys' view by the State House and moved out onto the lawn, she did her best to walk in a don't-care manner. In this way, she thought, if Bernard and David saw her, they would be convinced they were not at all on her mind.

Still trying to maintain her easy stride, she cut at an angle across to Senate Street and through the backyards of Marion Street to her house.

Jeff and Michael were still hammering away at their tree house, and her mom was not yet home. Beelzebub was in his usual spot on the kitchen window ledge. Jill leaned over her mom's red geranium bed and stretched to give Beelzebub a kiss on the nose. Beelzebub twisted his tail about, purred, and opened his eyes to show thin green slits. Jill thought of how Rod was always saying she and Beelzebub had eyes that were alike.

"Bee," Jill said softly as she gave herself a little push to regain her balance, "if you didn't stay out so late, you wouldn't have to sleep all day."

At least the house was quiet for a change. Larry was probably working at his job at the gas station. Jill couldn't help thinking how much nicer he'd been to her since he'd gotten a job and a girl friend. Maybe one day Rod would do the same. He was forever finding out things she didn't want him to know and running them in the ground. He was most likely with Dad right now at their garden plot just outside town.

Jill poured herself a glass of milk, grabbed some cheese and crackers, and went up to her room. *Mom is right*, she thought, *this place is a mess.* After finding a spot to set her glass, she opened the door of the closet and started dragging things out. She had found that when she was angry, it was a good time to clean. She wasn't so sentimental then and would get rid of lots of the junk that cluttered her room.

Jill worked away, not realizing Beelzebub was at her

45

window until she heard his scratch on the screen. "So there was no one to let you in downstairs, huh?" She leaned over and let him in.

Beelzebub jumped from the window ledge onto Jill's bed and began to search for the right spot to lie down.

"Dad's right. He says you're a noctural animal because you're always roaming at night and sleeping in the daytime."

With a shudder, Jill supposed that ghosts were nocturnal too.

As she stuffed the *no-good* papers in a trash can and straightened her closet shelves, she decided that for the time being at least she would put David and Bernard and their ghost completely out of her mind.

V.

The Class Tour

On Monday when the trio climbed down from the city transit, they knew that today was the day their class would go to the Capitol. The school band's yellow bus was already waiting for them in the parking lot.

"Shoot!" said David above the chatter around them. "I wish they'd let us walk to the Capitol instead of riding on that old bus."

"You know they'd never do that," said Jill. "We might pinch somebody's shrubbery along the way." She was over her anger with David and Bernard, and she was glad to see David as friendly as ever. She had avoided them the rest of Saturday, and on Sunday had gone to church with her family. For a special treat her dad had taken them all—all, that is, but Larry who'd gone off with his girl friend—out to dinner and then to Riverbanks Zoo.

Anyway, how could she keep from talking to David

on the bus this morning when she had so much to tell him?

By now the two of them were accustomed to Bernard's unawareness of what was going on about him. Either he was lost in his thoughts, or he just didn't have a sense of humor. As yet Jill hadn't figured it out.

Time scooted by much more quickly than Jill thought it would, and before they knew it, the high-spirited class was boarding the bus.

"I wish I'd brought a pad and pencil," said Jill looking around at some of the other girls with shoulder bags swinging at their hips. Jill had never liked carrying a pocketbook. "We'll never remember everything," she added.

"I still don't think that's the thing to do," said David as they found seats on the bus. He lowered his voice. "We don't want to look suspicious." For once Jill refrained from answering. There was no need for another argument to flare up. "Anyway," he concluded, "we've got Bernard."

Miss Maynard clapped her hands at the front of the bus to gain attention and give last-minute instructions about staying with the group and displaying nice manners.

Once at the State House, they spilled out of the bus and onto the familiar grounds.

Following the visitors' tour signs, they entered a side door on the ground floor. Just ahead, the security guards' desk jutted out into the wide corridor. Everything seemed massive and the lighting was unusual, with daylight entering only at each end of the long hall-like room. An eerie feeling crept over Jill. She turned toward David to hear him give a soft whistle through his teeth.

She knew what he was thinking.

Miss Maynard stopped and turned toward her group. "This was once the entrance of the Capitol," she said. Then she led them up several steps into a large lobby and crossed over to a desk marked VISITORS' INFORMATION.

A nice lady with smiling eyes greeted them and ushered the group to the center of the big room to begin the tour.

The guide introduced herself and began, "You are now in the third South Carolina State House. The first one was in Charleston; the second, a wooden building, was burned during the Civil War; and this one, which was begun in 1855, was shelled in 1865 during the Civil War from across the Congaree River. When you go outside, you will see six brass markers denoting the spots where the cannon balls hit."

Jill looked at Bernard. He was squinting up at the arched brick ceiling that had been painted white. She wondered if he remembered that they were supposed to be studying the layout of the building. As she had tried to tell him, it would be hard to find their way around at night, even if they knew it well.

"Now the granite in this building," continued their smiling guide, "was quarried in South Carolina. In fact, it came from within four miles of here. This is the original floor of the building and has been in use over one hundred years. The white marble you're standing on came from the state of Georgia, and the pink from Tennessee."

When the sweet-faced guide started talking about the Doric architecture over the entrances to the governor's and lieutenant governor's offices, Jill knew they'd better get down to business.

Careful not to get Miss Maynard upset with her about whispering while the guide was talking, she edged closer to David and tried to communicate in sign language. She could tell David got her message, but she still wished she had brought something to write on.

From the lower lobby, they climbed broad steps to a landing that led to the main lobby. Here, in what the guide called a rotunda, was a red carpet with the design of an eagle woven into it. The guide pointed out that the decorator had been granted a patent on the design so it could not be used anywhere else. Jill would have to remember to tell her mother that.

Her eyes were racing over the railed balcony that ran around the sides and back of the huge room when she noticed the heads of her classmates craning back and up. Instinctively she looked up too and found herself gazing into the large inner dome. *So this is where the noises come from!*

Lights shone through from somewhere above, giving the impression of a still larger area beyond. Jill had been in the State House many times, but never before had it made such an impression on her. She looked for David, made her way through the group, and wriggled in beside him. Poking her elbow in his ribs, she whispered, "How do you get up there?"

"Ask her," he whispered back.

Jill stuck her hand up immediately even though the guide was in the middle of a sentence. But before she could ask her question, the guide said, "No one is allowed in the dome except repairmen and maintenance men. There are unfinished attics so it's quite dangerous. Of course," she added, "the person responsible for raising and lowering the flag must also go into the dome."

"How tall is it?" a girl asked.

"It's one hundred and eighty feet from the top of the dome to the ground," the guide answered.

"How do you get up there?" another voice asked, and Jill shot David a thankful glance.

"The entrance is from the balcony, near the desk there by the oval window." The guide pointed in that direction and heads turned. "Of course," she added quickly, "that door is always kept locked."

Of course! Jill's hopes fell.

Where is that Bernard? Why isn't he paying attention? she thought in irritation, taking her frustrations out on him.

Then she spotted him in the center of the lobby peering into the face of John C. Calhoun's statue.

"Note the painting on the wall behind you," the guide said, and Miss Maynard patted shoulders and pointed to the large battle scene above the steps. "That is a reenactment of the surrender of the Tories in 1860. Here, we have Francis Marion, who was known as the Swamp Fox, protecting a Tory from his own troops who wanted to hang him because he had surrendered."

"Are these trees real?" a tall girl near Jill asked, and Miss Maynard frowned at her for touching one of the large palmetto trees in the lobby.

"Yes," the lady replied, "they are real. They came from Hunting Island on the coast of South Carolina. Naturally they wouldn't live on the inside so they were taken apart and each piece preserved. Then the pieces were wired together exactly as they grew."

"I've read," said Bernard, "that people in Florida eat the leaf bud of the palmetto tree."

51

"That's right," the guide said. "It has a cabbage-like taste."

Somebody said "Ugh!" as the guide continued. "But we in South Carolina don't use it for food or other purposes because it's our state tree.

"Now be sure when you go outside," the guide went on, "to look at the artificial tree on the grounds. It looks so real it even fools the birds. Some build their nests in the fronds in the spring."

By the time they were ushered into the library, Jill was totally confused. *How would they know where all these doors led at night?*

The guide explained that this was not a lending library as they were accustomed to, but that it was a law library containing acts, codes, and journals. It also served, she said, as the office of the Legislative Council. . . . *Whatever that is*, Jill thought.

The guide went on to say that the chandeliers of Venetian glass were once fueled with gas, but were now electrified.

Jill liked the wrought-iron steps best. She wished they had been allowed to go up them, but there were so many people busily working she supposed their traipsing by would be a disturbance.

From the library they continued upstairs to the Senate chamber, which contained the long, heavy desks of South Carolina's forty-six senators. The guide told them about the portraits hanging on the chamber walls. For once Jill wished she had Bernard's mind. How would it feel to remember everything you heard? she wondered.

Jill turned toward the guide who was pointing to a portrait and saying, ". . . the only lady whose likeness stands in the State House."

"What was her name again?" Jill asked.

"Ann Pamela Cunningham," the guide enunciated carefully. "It was she who was responsible for preserving Mt. Vernon, George Washington's home."

Well, Jill thought, *I hope Bernard and David took that in!*

It was then that Jill noticed the eyes in the portrait over the Senate rostrum. The guide said it was John C. Calhoun, again. Jill drew her eyes away from his. *Did he know what they were up to?*

Before Jill could stop herself, she asked, "Are there any ghosts in the Capitol?"

Everybody gasped or giggled, and Miss Maynard shushed them.

The guide looked somewhat puzzled before she said, "Oh, we don't circulate rumors like that." For a brief moment she lost her smile. Then she added, "We want tourists and visitors to come to our Capitol; we don't want to scare them away."

Jill wouldn't let herself look at David. He was probably furious with her for asking. But now they had an even better reason for wanting to exorcise the ghost. They would be helping the whole image of South Carolina—the guide had said so herself.

"Now I know all of you are familiar with the State Seal," the guide said, pointing to where it hung above the heavy Senate desk. "John Rutledge authorized the designing of this seal for South Carolina in 1776. On the arms side you see a palmetto tree growing on the seashore. This symbolizes the fort on Sullivan's Island because it was built of palmetto logs. The oak tree lying at its base stands for the British fleet because their ships were constructed of oak timbers.

53

"And, of course," she went on, "the British were defeated at Fort Moultrie on Sullivan's Island. The small shields hanging just below the palmetto branches display two important dates: March 26, the date of the ratification of the Constitution of South Carolina, and July 4, the date of the Declaration of Independence. Down near the bottom you see the year 1776.

"The twelve spears," she continued, "that are bound to the stem of the palmetto represent the twelve states that first became a part of the Union. And most importantly, the seal bears a Latin inscription, *Animis Opibusque Parati*, which means 'Prepared in mind and resources.' That is our State Motto."

"Gosh!" somebody exclaimed. "Who can remember all that?"

"Bernard," a voice from the back volunteered.

"Now the other side," explained the tour guide, "is not so involved. It has, as you see, a woman walking on the seashore. Upon closer observation you can see she's walking over swords and daggers. This, with the beginning of the sunrise in the background, signifies hope overcoming dangers. In one hand she has the laurel branch, symbolizing the victory won at Sullivan's Island, and in the other she holds a robe. The inscription on this side reads *Dum Spiro Spero*, meaning 'While I breath, I hope.'"

"That says a lot," a voice in the group declared.

"It surely does," responded the guide, and Jill was amazed that she was still smiling. "So you see, if you study your State Seal and understand what everything on it represents, you'll really know a great deal of South Carolina history."

"You can say that again." The minute Jill said it, she

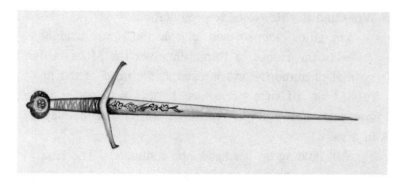

knew she shouldn't have used that expression with the guide, so she purposefully avoided Miss Maynard's gaze.

"And last," the guide said, "is the Sword of State." She pointed to a glass-enclosed case in front of the rostrum. "It rests in this rack during the daily sessions of the Senate and is carried by the sergeant at arms on all state occasions. This sword was presented to the Senate in 1951 by Lord Halifax, a British ambassador to the United States. It is etched with the State Flower, the yellow jessamine, and has the State Seal engraved on it."

"Wasn't your first sword taken?" asked Bernard.

"Yes, it was, young man. It *disappeared* in 1941. It was the state's oldest relic and there are still no clues to its whereabouts. For ten years the Senate used a cavalry sword in its place, but now that has been returned to the Charleston Museum."

As she spoke, the guide picked up an iron rod. She placed it in the rack prepared for the sword. Lights at either end of the rostrum came on. "This," she explained, "is where the sword stays while laws are being passed. Now if you will file by as you leave the chamber, you can get a closer look at the sword."

They marched single file by the glass-enclosed sword and followed one another across the balcony to the West

Wing and the House of Representatives.

The guide stopped them outside the House chamber. "Now in the House of Representatives the Mace is the symbol of authority and is used at the head of the procession on all state occasions. It, too, was stolen several years ago but was recovered and is now displayed in a vault."

Still holding up her hand, she continued, "The House is in session. You may go into the balcony and observe as long as you wish."

Miss Maynard began thanking the guide, and many members of the class joined in thanking her too. Everybody seemed pleased as they started into the already crowded viewing area.

Joggling on the bus back to school, Jill felt disappointed. As far as she was concerned, the tour hadn't helped them that much. Besides, the guide said the dome was kept locked. So even if they managed to get inside the Capitol, they wouldn't be able to get into the dome.

Would they have to? After all, what did this exorcising, or whatever Bernard called it, involve? How close did you have to get to a ghost to do that? Jill was more confused than ever.

Miss Maynard must have known they wouldn't be able to settle down after their return from the field trip. So for the afternoon she had planned a project she called a relief map of South Carolina. With a mixture of flour, water, and food coloring, they would form the hills, valleys, and rivers of their state.

At first Miss Maynard had assigned Jill to the group working on the Blue Ridge Mountain region, but she had begged to work on the Piedmont Plateau section.

Already she had begun to feel that the Capitol was part hers, and she wanted to be in on placing the dot on the map that would represent it.

Jill went to the library with two others to do research. It was important that they place the rivers exactly right.

David, she noticed, was in the same group as Bernard. They had been assigned to the Coastal Plain, and the others in their group had sent Bernard to the library to do their research while they stayed behind to get their moist concoction ready.

Jill had wanted to get David's and Bernard's reactions to the tour as they left the Capitol Building, but there hadn't been a chance with all the other students around.

Now everyone was so engrossed in the relief map they didn't even want to take their break. Still, Jill found the thought of the Capitol's ghost edging its way into her thoughts every now and then. With the promise of an afternoon of planning with David and Bernard, she kept edging it out again.

VI.

The Museum

Occasionally during the map project, Jill looked at David and Bernard. Were they thinking of their ghost? If they were, their faces showed no sign of it.

After boarding the bus for home, she made her way to the vacant seat in front of David and turned sideways. "What did you think of it?" she asked.

"What did I think of what?"

"The tour, dummy. What else?"

"I thought the question you asked the guide about a ghost in the Capitol was great, Jill—just great," he chided, careful not to let his expression indicate his scorn.

"You know, David Peoples, you're getting more like Bernard every day."

"Thanks. I'll take that as a compliment." He looked around the now-crowded bus. "Where is old brainchild anyway?"

"Right behind the driver. Where else?"

"Listen, Jill." David leaned closer to her, his voice serious. "We need Bernard."

"Yeah. Yeah. I never said I didn't like him."

"Besides," said David, "he's taking us to the museum this afternoon. He thinks there might be some clue there."

"Really? I'll have to go home first."

"Me too. I told him we'd meet him there as soon as we could."

That afternoon when David and Jill entered the museum, Bernard was talking to the gray-haired lady at the desk.

"These must be your friends now, Bernard," the lady said, smiling.

"Mrs. Smith," Bernard said, "this is Jill Johnston and David Peoples."

"I'm delighted for young people to come in on their own," Mrs. Smith said. "You know, we have school youngsters come in groups, and we're glad to have them." She lowered her voice. "But confidentially, most of them are not that interested in the history of their state." Then she laughed. "They do enjoy time off from their studies."

Jill looked at David. Did he feel guilty, she wondered. If they weren't trying to track down clues to their ghost, they would likely not be here either.

Mrs. Smith stood up and right away Jill noticed how well-groomed she was—"as neat as a pin," Aunt Becky would say.

"Now just browse around and enjoy yourselves. If there are any questions, let me know," she said as she entered a small room at the rear of the museum.

Starting on the left side, they first viewed the spinning wheels. Then David called attention to an old powder horn made from a gourd that dated from 1834. In the next exhibit, they looked at canteens, cannon balls, and a cow horn.

When she was certain Mrs. Smith couldn't hear her, Jill whispered, "What do you hope to find here, Bernard?"

"I'm not sure," he croaked back. "Keep looking. This place is filled with old Civil War relics, and if that *is* our period of time, there may be something here."

"And what if we do find something?" asked David. "Then what?"

"Mrs. Smith is a friend of mine," explained Bernard, making every effort to keep his voice low. "We'll work something out."

"You mean you'll tell her?"

"Not of our plans to exorcise the ghost—no."

Jill looked at David to study his reaction to what Bernard had said about *exorcising* the ghost. She wished Bernard wouldn't use that word. In the first place, Jill still didn't understand exactly what it meant and that made it all the more frightening. Tonight she would look it up.

They moved on to some display cases with soldiers' uniforms, a carpet bag from Reconstruction days, and letters in old-fashioned spidery writing.

On the right side of the room, tall glass enclosures held figures of important men in history. Bernard pointed out Robert Mills. "He's my favorite. Did you know he was the architect for the Washington Monument?"

"David probably knew it," answered Jill somewhat sarcastically, "but I didn't." She sighed. Was Bernard

60

going to start up again with all this history stuff that had absolutely nothing to do with what they were trying to accomplish?

"I knew there was a house on Blanding Street called the Robert Mills House," said David, "but I didn't know about the Washington Monument thing. Is that why he's famous?"

"Yes—because he was an architect for many United States Presidents."

Jill was glad to see Mrs. Smith coming toward them. She had already bitten her tongue too hard trying to keep from telling Bernard again to skip the parts that didn't have anything to do with their plans.

"You know," Mrs. Smith said, "this monring I had some employees at the Capitol bring over some boxes that we had stored there. Evidently they overlooked one, for I know there was a little box with odd buttons and such. We use them for repairs."

"Want us to get it for you?" asked David.

Mrs. Smith looked at her watch. "It's almost closing time. I really don't think anyone else will be coming in. Perhaps you would like to walk over with me, and you young men can take turns bringing the box back."

"To the Capitol?" asked Jill almost too enthusiastically. "Yes ma'am."

"Yes," said Mrs. Smith. "You know the museum used to be in the State House. But we were so crowded there. That's why we had some unidentified articles stored in the tunnel."

"I've heard about the tunnel under the Capitol," exclaimed David. "You mean we get to go in it?"

"I'm sure the security guards won't mind. The yard

crews will have gone by now. They keep their tools there." She looked at her watch again. "Yes, this will probably be a good time to go."

Jill felt her excitement mounting. Even if they didn't find any clues, it would be a real treat to get in the tunnel. In short order the three of them crossed Sumter Street with Mrs. Smith and headed toward the Capitol grounds.

"You know," Mrs. Smith said, turning her head slightly as she spoke so that Bernard and David, who were walking behind them, could hear, "it was a tragedy that South Carolina lost so many of her valuable collections during the Civil War."

"We talked about that the other day with Aunt Becky," Bernard told her.

"There was a Dr. Gibbes—Dr. Robert Gibbes," Mrs. Smith continued, "who had one of the finest coin collections anywhere, not to speak of his fine art and literary works that included many letters written during the American Revolution."

"And," her voice became excited, "something I'm sure you all would have liked—a cabinet of Southern fossils, including sharks' teeth."

"I have a necklace made of sharks' teeth from Myrtle Beach," said Jill.

"I doubt they're very famous, Jill," remarked David.

"They might be someday," she retorted, refusing to be outdone.

"That's right," said Mrs. Smith. "Now you're talking like a future museum curator."

"Not me," Jill responded. "Bernard could be one."

"Yes," agreed Mrs. Smith. "Bernard is my most faithful visitor."

62

"Were the collections burned when Sherman came through?" asked David, remembering their discussion with Aunt Becky.

"Yes, they were," answered Mrs. Smith. "The soldiers came into his house and set fire to the lace curtains." She looked sad. "And I understand Dr. Gibbes was such a kind man."

For once Jill forgot not to be interested in any history that wasn't connected with their ghost. She was listening so intently she didn't realize they had already reached the East Entrance of the State House.

They followed as Mrs. Smith went up to the security guard at the center desk, identified herself, and asked if she might go into the tunnel to see if the missing box was there.

The officer switched on his walkie-talkie and summoned another guard.

Jill couldn't help thinking how much she'd have to tell her family tonight. Her brothers would be envious.

They followed the uniformed guard outside and down to the lower level.

"Mmmmm. Smell the yellow jessamine," said Mrs. Smith, taking a deep breath.

"Yeah," said the guard. "Fragrant, isn't it? You no-

63

tice they've planted it all around the Capitol now." His keys jingled as he opened the heavy tunnel door. The damp, cool underground smell engulfed them. "Do you know where they were stored?" he asked.

"They were in the little room nearest the exit from the Governor's office," Mrs. Smith explained.

"You mean the tunnel leads to the Governor's office?" asked David. "That's neat!"

"That must be so he can make a quick getaway," quipped Jill, and they all laughed.

"I see this serves as a fallout shelter," said Bernard, pointing out the little triangular sticker on the wall.

"Yes," said the guard. "That came about during the Cuban missile crisis."

"Does it go all the way under the Capitol?" asked David.

"It does now," the guard replied, "but when it was built, it didn't."

As they made their way along the molding passageway, Jill noticed the cleaning tools and supplies along the walls.

"I see there are intercommunication devices down here," said Bernard.

The guard laughed. "Yes, the whole place is bugged. There's not much you can get away with around here."

"Even the dome is bugged?" asked Jill.

David gave her a *there-you-go-again* look as the guard said, "Most especially the dome."

"There it is," said Mrs. Smith, pointing ahead and walking into a small opened room. She stooped down before a cardboard box with MUSEUM printed on it in bold black letters. "I wonder how it could have been overlooked," she mused.

"You'd be surprised at some of the help we have around here," the guard said, shaking his head.

"Oh, well, we should have moved all of this long ago. Had it any value, I'm sure we would have."

"With all the old legislative files stored down here," the guard offered, "I'm sure your little boxes haven't bothered anyone."

Jill couldn't help thinking how nice the guard was. This was the second guard she had met and liked. She hated having to trick people she was fond of. But there would be no other way they could get into the Capitol at night. A creepy shiver passed over her again.

"Now," said Mrs. Smith, "if you fellows will just lift this carton onto the table we'll see if the little mending box is in here."

"Tell you what," said the guard. "I'll just put the exit door on lock, so when you come out just make sure it's closed tight."

Mrs. Smith thanked him as David and Bernard hoisted the box onto the table. A musty smell of old paper and cloth exuded from it.

The three were all eyes as Mrs. Smith opened the cardboard box and began to lift out its contents.

"Now these old postcards," she said, "are really not old enough to be valuable, but we hated to discard them."

The smell of wool permeated the air as she unfolded an old blue uniform.

"What's that Union outfit doing in here?" asked Bernard.

"There were lots of these found around," she said, "but no one knows whom they belonged to." She reached under some old papers. "Here it is—the mending box I was looking for."

They all leaned forward as Mrs. Smith opened a small cigar box. Jill saw some tarnished finger rings and pins, a little pair of rusted scissors, buttons, and scraps of old-looking material. It reminded her of her own little junk box on her closet shelf at home.

Mrs. Smith was pushing the contents around with her slender finger when Jill spied a lock of hair on the table beside the box. "Look," she said, pointing to it, "there's somebody's hair!"

Jill's and David's eyes met. *Aunt Becky had said the Southern girl had given her lover a picture of herself and a lock of her golden hair.* It was golden all right, or it had been, and it was tied with a faded ribbon. Jill's eyes darted from David to Bernard and back again.

Mrs. Smith picked up the lock of hair and turned it over in her hand. "Why, it must have fallen from the uniform I just took out," she said. "How odd. I don't remember its being there."

For a moment they all just stood there staring at it until Mrs. Smith said, "And it must have been beautiful once."

"And you don't have any idea whose it was?" asked Bernard.

"No—sadly, we don't. That's why these things were stored down here. Unless they can be identified, they have no significance for a museum. We must have proof of their authenticity, you understand. There can be no guesswork."

Jill found her voice. "What will you do with these things?"

"Oh, I suppose we'll just continue to stick them back some place and rummage through when we need a but-

ton or such for mending."

"What about the hair?" asked Jill.

"I'm afraid if it hasn't been identified after all these years, it never will be. I can't tell you how many knowledgeable persons have gone through all these contents—many times."

Jill summoned every ounce of courage in her body before she said, "Mrs. Smith, could we . . . could I have the lock of hair?"

All the eyes in the room seemed to penetrate her until Mrs. Smith spoke. "Well," she said slowly, "I suppose you could, Jill. Of course the museum property is not mine to dispose of—it belongs to the state of South Carolina. . . . But, yes, you may have the lock of hair. Besides, if the uniform couldn't be traced, I'm sure the lock of hair could not be either."

From then on, the events of the afternoon ran to-

67

gether for Jill. She was so excited over having the lock of hair she could hardly stand it. If the hair was that given to the Northern soldier, then that uniform in the museum box must have been his. But who was he? Aunt Becky hadn't known.

With every glance at David, she could tell he was pleased as punch over the find, and she imagined that Bernard was too. Was the ghost that was haunting the Capitol really looking for this lock of hair? Had he known it was there somewhere? Jill couldn't believe they'd really found a clue.

The sun was low by the time they dropped the box off at the museum. Jill knew she'd better hurry home. Not once had she let go of the lock of hair. For fear she'd lose it, she didn't even put it in her pocket.

With hurried plans to get together the next afternoon and make final arrangements, and with a strict caution from David and Bernard not to lose the lock of hair, Jill raced across the back lot to her house.

As usual Beelzebub was resting on his ledge at the kitchen window. Jill leaned to give him a quick kiss. In her rush, she lost her balance and almost fell onto her mother's geraniums. Quickly she brought up the hand clutching the hair and steadied herself.

Without apparent reason, Beelzebub hissed. His black hair stood like wire as he streaked across the geranium bed and shot up the nearest tree.

"Good grief!" exclaimed Jill, amazed at Beelzebub's actions.

"Jill!" her mother called. "Is that you? Hurry—dinner."

"Well," her father said as he came into the dining room, "I hear you've been to the museum."

"The museum?" asked Michael. "Whatever for?"

"Mrs. Smith gave me this because they don't know whose it was," said Jill holding up the lock of hair.

"Somebody's who's dead?" croaked Rod. "Ugh! Where you gonna keep it?"

"All right," said Mrs. Johnston. "Close your eyes for the blessing, and we can go ahead while Jill washes up."

During dinner Jill told her family about the class tour of the Capitol, the relief map of South Carolina they were making at school, and the visit to the tunnel. Even Bobby listened. For once she was the center of attention. All the while, though, she had to be careful not to tell about the ghost and the plans involving him. Jill knew her father well enough to know he would put a stop to any ideas they might have about entering the Capitol after dark.

Jill had no homework, which was a rare treat, and she was thankful. Today had been wonderful, but it had been exhausting too. She helped her mother clear the dishes and headed for her room.

Once there, she tiptoed to reach her treasure box on the top shelf of her closet. That would be a safe place for the hair until they made their plans. For a while Jill looked through her trinkets and keepsakes. She lifted an arrowhead she had found several years ago and sat fingering it. She liked its smoothness. . . . If only these things could talk. . . .

She was about to crawl into bed when she remembered that she wanted to look up the word *exorcise*. She pulled her dictionary from the bottom shelf of her bedside table, flipped to the *ex* section, found her word, and began to read: *to seek to expel an evil spirit by ritual prayers or solemn ceremonies.*

69

"Gosh! I don't understand that. Bernard said he was a good ghost. If he's good, how could he be evil?" She'd just have to ask Bernard about that!

Jill snapped off her light and turned over onto her side. She could hear the TV going downstairs.

A scratching on the screen caught her attention, and Jill leaned over to let Beelzebub in. In the semi-darkness, she waited to feel the soft body slip by her hand. But Beelzebub did not come in.

"Come on, Bee," she coaxed. Jill leaned farther toward the window. The street light gleamed silver on the shingled roof, but Beelzebub was nowhere in sight.

That's peculiar, Jill thought. She pressed the screen into place again and lay back in her bed. Then with a jolt she sat up, realizing how strangely Beelzebub had reacted when she brought the lock of hair close to him outside the kitchen window.

What was it Jill had heard—that cats can smell death and they won't stay around where somebody has died? Could it be that he could tell the hair belonged to a dead person?

For as long as Jill could remember, people had made remarks about her black cat and bad luck and witches and such, but she had always taken it in fun as she'd thought they meant it to be. But now, she wondered— had they been serious?

A sudden breeze chilled her. She pulled up the thin sheet and tucked it tightly around her body. If Bee had come in, she would have lowered her window.

Jill was bothered by something else too. Had the men from the State House *really* overlooked the box? It had been so obvious—right there on the floor and with the word MUSEUM written on it. . . . Or, was there another reason they had left it behind? Had something peculiar taken place that caused them not to want to carry it?

Jill raised her head off her pillow. She heard a muffled sound like that of someone walking. She waited. . . . It grew louder. . . . She thought it might have been one of her brothers. . . . But, the strange thing was, *it didn't sound like it was inside. It sounded like someone moving over the roof outside her gabled window.* . . . At length, it grew faint and then she could hear it no more.

Jill went cold from head to foot. Had the ghost come here? The lock of hair had been in the Capitol and so had the ghost!

Then an odd thing happened. Jill began to feel light as if she were floating about in space. She wanted to get out of bed and go down to her mother's room, but her arms and legs felt weightless and she didn't know how to move them. And what would she tell her mother if she were able to get down to her? Just this once, she wished her older brothers were already in their rooms and close-by. . . . *Where is that trifling cat?* she thought suddenly. *His warm body would be a comfort.*

As quickly as it had come, the weird sensation disappeared. Maybe she had been dreaming. Sometimes that happened—especially when she was tired.

Jill drew a long nervous breath and buried her head under the pillow.

VII.

Reconnoiter

"All right," said Bernard the next afternoon as they sat on the Capitol grounds near the James F. Byrnes statue, "this venture is going to take a great deal of knowledgeable planning and reconnoitering."

"That first thing," said Jill, "is what we have you for, Bernard, and the second—well, whatever it means—we're all in this together."

"You dummy, Jill," said David. "It means *looking around*. I learned that in Scouts."

"Me a dummy?" scoffed Jill. "Who got the lock of hair?"

As she spoke the skin on her arms turned to gooseflesh. She hadn't told David and Bernard about Beelzebub's reaction to the lock of hair and the peculiar sensations she'd had in bed last night. They would just say she was scared. But she knew that wasn't it. The floating part could have been a dream. Today at school when they were so happily working on the relief map, she was sure it was. But why did Bee not come home last night? And she hadn't seen him at all today.

"Jill," said David, jogging her out of her daydreams, "Bernard asked if you could get out of your house at midnight."

"Well, gosh, I guess so if you two can. Does it *have* to be done at night?"

"Yes," said Bernard, "the ritual has to be done when the spirit is active, and that means at night."

"I guess I can sneak out," she said. "What about you, David?"

"You know what Aunt Becky says, 'Where there's a will, there's a way.'"

"Yeah," said Jill, "but I don't think she was talking about anything like this. Anyway, you could just say you were spending the night with Bernard."

"Nawh, I don't want to tell Grandma a lie about it. Sneaking into the Capitol is going to be bad enough."

"But you really could spend the night with him—what's left of it."

"Why don't *you* stay overnight with somebody?" David asked her.

"Now that *would* look kinda funny—for me to spend the night with Bernard—don't you think?"

"Don't you know any girls?" asked Bernard.

"Sure, I know some girls. But they don't live near the Capitol, and even if they did, I don't want to spend the night with any of them."

"How about you, Bernard?" David asked. "What'll you tell your parents?"

"No problem," he said in his monotone. "They probably won't even be at home."

"You mean they leave you there by yourself?" asked Jill.

"The clerk keeps an eye on me when they need to go somewhere."

"Yeah, so I gathered," Jill said, remembering the clerk in the lobby who had told her Bernard would be at the Capitol or the museum.

"Okay, then," directed Bernard, "each one is responsible for working out his own pattern for meeting on this spot at twelve o'clock Friday night."

"This Friday night?" asked Jill. On second thought, she didn't know why she had asked the question. It seemed so close, but she wasn't sure she could take three more nights with the lock of hair in her room.

Jill's outburst seemed to need no answer.

"So much for Stage I," said Bernard.

"But *how* are we going to get into the Capitol?" Jill asked.

"That's Stage II," replied Bernard, "and we're open for suggestions right now."

"It's too bad we can't get in the tunnel and go up through the Governor's office," said David.

"Oh, we could never open those thick tunnel doors," said Bernard. "It's a fallout shelter—remember? Besides, it's my guess that the door won't open from the tunnel into his office. That would be too dangerous. It's probably just an exit."

"I guess so," David agreed.

"I've given some thought to going in earlier in the afternoon and hiding and then letting you two in at midnight," said Bernard.

"Say—that's a good idea!" Jill perked up. "David

and I could never get away with that. Mom would have my brothers swarming over this area like flies, and David's grandmother would have the police out searching for him. But you could do it, Bernard."

Jill had grown so accustomed to Bernard's habit of accenting his speech with his hands that she hardly noticed it as he continued. "As I said, I've given it thought and decided upon it only as a last resort."

"Don't tell me you're scared!" Jill scorned.

"No, it isn't that. It's just that I don't want to have to crouch in the dark that long without being able to read."

"That figures," retorted Jill, not doubting his word.

David leaned up on his elbow and studied the State House. "The easiest thing would be to find an unlocked window."

"We won't be able to do that," stated Bernard. "That's primarily what security guards do—go around checking windows and doors."

"I know!" exclaimed Jill, getting up on her knees. "We could go in Friday afternoon, just as visitors, and I could unlock that window on the lower level—the one there by the steps."

"Shhhhhhh," David said, leaning over and grabbing her finger, which was pointing toward the Capitol. "Who all are you telling?" he asked, gesturing toward the pedestrians behind them waiting to cross Gervais Street.

"How would you manage that with the office workers still inside?" Bernard asked.

"I could go in about closing time and—" Jill's thoughts raced on almost faster than she could express them. "You remember the day we toured the Capitol— well, there was a pretty, dark-haired lady who had a desk over by the front window. I could start talking to her while she's tidying up her desk. She would never know!"

"What do you think, David?" asked Bernard.

"And who'd crawl in the window that night?"

"All of us, I guess," said Bernard. "We couldn't take a chance of trying to open any doors."

For a moment they were quiet. Jill's arms were again rippled with gooseflesh. "Let's go take a closer look," she said, standing up.

"Wait a minute!" David yelled. "We'll blow the whole thing snooping around windows."

"I agree," said Bernard. "The thing to do is walk around nonchalantly."

"Oh, Bernard," Jill said, running her fingers through her hair. "If you use all those big words Friday night, the ghost won't even know you're trying to get him to leave."

"He means to act like we aren't interested in the window, Jill," explained David.

Jill was already several steps ahead. After all, hadn't she been the one who made the suggestion to go through the window? And didn't she have the lock of hair? She wasn't going to let their *know-it-all* airs bother her one little bit.

As they strolled quietly by the appointed window, Jill noticed that it didn't have a screen. There was no need for one in the air-conditioned building. But it looked as if it hadn't been opened in ages. It might even be nailed shut.

"All right," said Bernard when they had gone around the far side of the Capitol and settled themselves in the sun-flecked shadows at the base of Wade Hampton's

statue. "Stage II can be considered tentative, and we can go on to Stage III."

Jill caught the edge of her tongue between her teeth and looked at Bernard. She wouldn't give him the satisfaction of knowing he had used another word she didn't know. Obviously it meant just continue with their plan to go in the window unless they found out it wouldn't work. In that case, Bernard would hide in the building.

"I think," said David, "we'll have to wait until we get inside to make up our minds as to how we're going to get in the dome. It'll depend on where the guards are."

"Do we have to go in the dome?" asked Jill, knowing Bernard's response before she asked him.

"Yes," said Bernard. "That's where these spirits usually stay—in attics or some unused section of a building."

"But the guide on our tour said the door leading up to the dome was kept locked," said Jill. "Remember?"

"Maybe we could use a skeleton key," David said. "I've got bunches of old keys."

"We could try. But don't bring them all—they'd rattle and attract attention."

"Okay," agreed David. "I'll pick out the ones that look like they would fit old locks."

"How'll we be able to see once we get up there?" asked Jill.

"They always light up the dome at night, don't they?" asked David.

"Yes," said Bernard, "it's lit up at night. I imagine though it will be dim inside. But that's the way we need it."

78

"What all do you have to do?" Jill asked.

"I'm reading up on the ritual. It's in one of my father's books. All *you* have to do, though, is be sure to bring the piece of hair."

"Well, what I don't understand," she said, remembering the definition in the dictionary, "if this guy's not an evil spirit, why are we using that exorcising junk on him?"

"The word *exorcise* just means we're getting him to move out." Bernard demonstrated by extending his arms out from him. "I'm sure you've heard of guardian angels. No one would deny they were good spirits."

Yes, Jill thought, she had heard of guardian angels and fairy godmothers. And she remembered a story about a little girl who'd had food served on silver platters from out of nowhere. But would these people—or spirits—make ghostly noises and throw things? Maybe if the person they watched over was in danger, they would. Why did it all have to be so confusing?

"In fact," admitted Bernard, breaking into Jill's thoughts, "I haven't finished reading up on it yet. But I do know it won't be an involved ceremony like those used to cast out devil spirits. Actually, I don't think it will require much of a ritual at all. We will just try to find out if the lock of hair is what he's looking for."

"Let's be sure to get it straight," said David, "and not call any more spirits in."

They laughed, but it was not the happy kind of laughter. It was more like the chuckle of stage fright.

"Bernard—" Jill hesitated a moment. "Maybe you ought to tell your father and let him help us."

"Oh, no!" responded Bernard in a manner faster than he usually spoke. "My father would never do anything like this. He experiments with extrasensory perception, but I'm quite sure he wouldn't have anything to do with exorcising a spirit."

"Well," asked David, "what makes you think we can do it if he can't?"

"It isn't that he can't. He just wouldn't. In the first place, nobody would be given permission to do such a thing. You heard the tour guide say they wanted to keep it quiet. Therefore, my father couldn't afford to get involved—not in his position.

"Besides," Bernard went on, "as I said earlier, poltergeists have a fondness for young people. He'd probably be more cooperative with us."

"I see what you mean," said David.

But Jill wasn't at all sure that she saw what Bernard meant. In fact, it was all getting so complicated, she was beginning to have doubts as to whether they should even go through with it.

"Maybe we should talk it over with Aunt Becky," she suggested.

"Oh, I don't think so," said David. "If Bernard thinks it's not a good idea to get his father involved, then I don't think we ought to get Aunt Becky in on this either. Anyway, what if she'd tell us we shouldn't do it? Then what?"

"Well, okay." Jill didn't want Aunt Becky in hot water with David's grandmother. "It was just an idea. But," she added, "I hope this is the spirit that we think it is. If not, we could be in trouble."

"I have every reason to believe," said Bernard in his most confidential manner, "that we are dealing with a poltergeist who is on some unfulfilled mission. He will not be able to rest until some message has been sent or some deed accomplished."

Jill looked at David. His expression told her he was in perfect agreement with Bernard. "Don't forget, Jill, that we are doing the people of Columbia a big favor by ridding the Capitol of its ghost."

Somehow Jill had the feeling that David was trying to bolster his own confidence.

"You're absolutely right," said Bernard. "Because unless someone can get these kinds of ghosts to go peacefully, there is no way to get rid of them except to demolish the building they're haunting. And South Carolina certainly can't tear down the State House."

"Then we might as well go on home," said Jill somewhat dejectedly. She knew full well there was no backing out now.

The sinking sun looked like an orange ball as they got up to go their separate ways.

VIII.
Countdown

For the last few days, it seemed that nothing had gone right for Jill. She kept telling herself what Aunt Becky often said—that she had "just gotten up on the wrong side of the bed."

At school somebody in her map group had put too much water in the flour mixture and it didn't set hard. Overnight the Congaree River had run over half of Richland County. And they had been so careful in mixing the colors for the water, even making it have a realistic muddy hue.

"Aw, we'll just pretend it flooded," somebody said. But that hadn't suited Jill at all. She had never known the Congaree to flood.

Besides that, the afternoons had really dragged. Bernard had decided that they shouldn't hang around the Capitol any more until after the entry.

Then too, David didn't want them to go see Aunt

Becky for fear their plans would leak out and be foiled, or they might implicate her in some way.

To top it off, Beelzebub had been gone ever since the day he got a whiff of the lock of hair. Jill had even put out his most tempting liver dish, but there was no sign of him.

"Don't worry, Jill," her mom had said. "Just remember when he came to you he was a stray. That kind has a streak of wildness. He'll come back. You'll see."

Jill tried to feel better. She had heard it said that her mother was an optimist, so she figured her mom was just saying those things to cheer her up. She guessed her mother was called an optimist because she was young and cheerful—and most mothers with a houseful of kids didn't often appear too cheerful.

Seeing the worry on Jill's face, her mother had gently caught her around the neck and pulled their heads together. Whenever she did this, she always ended up with "My, how you've grown—almost as tall as I am."

In a way her mother's concern had been comforting, but it made Jill feel guilty. If only she could tell her mom that Bee had run away because of the lock of hair. Would she still think he'd come back? Jill didn't hide things from her mom—there had never been any need. But this was different. Telling her mom now would put a stop to everything, and David and Bernard would never forgive her.

If only the State House could keep the same security guards year after year, maybe the men would get used to the poltergeist, and his noises wouldn't bother them. But if course, that was impossible.

Most importantly, though, they had to help the poltergeist. Bernard had said these ghosts don't want to return and haunt a place, but they can't help themselves. If he was really the tortured sweetheart they thought he was, it was sad to think of all the years he had been trying to get someone to understand him.

At any rate, if they didn't hurry up and get this thing over with, Jill felt she was going to need somebody to exorcise her from all these feelings of guilt.

Then last night, Jill hadn't been able to get to sleep, and she'd gone to her brother Rod's room to find something to read. She knew he didn't like her to go in his room without asking, but he wasn't there and she remembered a book of ghost stories he had.

She had found it without any trouble and had read the weirdest things: that witches can dry up the blood of cows and raise storms and sometimes leave messages written in bat's blood. She had found out, too, that the toad, the screech owl, and a black cat were inseparable companions of a witch.

But the scariest story of all was the one about a woman who could turn herself into a cat. Whenever the moon was full, she would slip out of the house. Her husband knew something strange was going on, and he suspected she was meeting another man. But all he knew for sure was that he would wake up during the night and his wife would be gone, although he never heard her leave the house.

Determined to find out what was going on, one night he sat up all night long. As he waited groggily by their bedroom window with a shotgun in his hand, he saw movement in the bushes nearby. Whatever it was, it was not a person—he could tell that. In the moonlight, it looked more like some kind of mountain animal. In an attempt to scare it away, he raised his gun and shot.

Fully awake by now, he could tell that he had wounded the thing and he ran outside to take a look. What he saw was a large black cat whose paw had been shot and was bleeding. As he approached it, it ran, dragging the wounded limb through the brush.

Stunned, the man returned to the house. In the bedroom he found his wife lying on the bed moaning and writhing in pain. She had been shot in the leg.

Jill was so frightened when she finished that last story, that she got out of bed and hurried to return the book to Rod's room. The bedlight he was reading by was so small she didn't realize he was in the room until he spoke.

"Don't you know how to knock?" he quipped, and Jill nearly jumped out of her skin. She mumbled something about not knowing he was there, and he came back with a retort about her ripping off his books. Then he leaned over to see what book she had returned.

"Ah–ha!" he said. "So you *are* a witch and that's why you have a black cat! Tell me—do you cut off toads' heads and put them in your cauldron?"

Jill quickly turned to go as Rod called, "Shut my door. I don't want just anything coming in."

Jill hurried down the dim hall and back to the comforting light of her room. She was in no mood to battle with Rod tonight. But she was angry with him. He always knew just what to say to make her blood boil. If only she had waited till morning to return the book. But she hadn't wanted it in her room overnight. Having the lock of hair was bad enough.

She'd a mind to go down and tell her parents on Rod for calling her a witch. If she did, though, she'd have to explain that she had been reading his ghost story book, and that might lead to other things. Sometimes confessions came out at night when you didn't even mean for them to.

No, she just wouldn't tell her parents he had been "teasing" her, as they called it. Dad had told Jill many times that brothers didn't really mean all the things they taunted little sisters with. He ought to know, he said, because he had a younger sister. Jill happened to know that her dad dearly loved his sister Elizabeth who now lived in Virginia. But once Aunt Elizabeth had told her that when they were growing up, Dad made her walk three steps behind him when they went anywhere to-gether. Now that she thought about it, she and Rod had never had a fist fight the way she and Michael had. Sometimes, though, that seemed the best way to clear the air.

In spite of everything, Friday finally arrived. And at least one thing turned out right. This afternoon she had gone to the Capitol alone and succeeded in unlocking the window. In fact, it had been so easy, she couldn't believe it.

She had walked into the Capitol along with some scattered tourists and some men carrying attaché cases and gone right into the large room with all the desks of the different clerks and secretaries. Trying her best to look as if she were on an errand, she went up to the pretty, dark-haired lady by the window whom she had remembered seeing earlier.

Jill had waited for her to look up and then she asked, "Could you tell me if Miss Jacques works here?"

The lady looked as if she were thinking hard, but even before she spoke, Jill knew what her answer would be. For Jill knew there was no such person—that is, no

real person. Miss Jacques had been an imaginary lady that Jill used to visit when she was small and played with dolls. Jill hadn't really liked Miss Jacques—as she was always telling Jill how to feed and diaper her doll— but for some reason the name just popped into her head.

"No," the lady replied, "I don't believe I know of anyone by that name." She looked so sincere that Jill felt sorry for her. "But then I haven't been working here very long," she added. "You could ask at the main desk," she said, pointing to the center of the large room that was noisy with the click of typewriters and voices.

Then the lady's phone had rung. As she answered it, her chair swung around slightly. Jill turned toward the window under the pretense of looking out. She was surprised to find that the metal lock was just even with her mouth. She twitched her nose as if it itched, brought her hand up to scratch it, and with a quick hard twist, she unlocked the window.

Her mission accomplished, she worked up a smile, waved her hand at the lady, and left the room. Jill hoped the telephone conversation kept her from noticing that she did not go to the center desk.

Even though unlocking the window had been easy, it had made Jill rather nervous. As she left the Capitol, she had an odd feeling that somebody was watching and would yell for her to come back and own up to what she had done.

When she got home, her mom was making supper and Bobby was in the backyard whining because he couldn't climb up into the tree fort with Michael and Jeff.

As soon as Jill made a quick secretive call to David to tell him "the mission was accomplished," she offered to take care of Bobby for her mom. As they walked around the block, Jill told Bobby they'd look for Beelzebub, and all along the way Bobby peeked under bushes calling "Come kitty, nice kitty!" But Beelzebub was nowhere to be seen.

When they were in sight of David's house, Jill had them turn around and start back. Aunt Becky would probably be sitting by her window, and Jill wouldn't want her to see them pass by without stopping. This was the longest she had ever gone without visiting Aunt Becky.

After dinner, Jill helped her mom with the dishes and watched television. All the while she kept getting up to see the clock or asking someone to tell her what time it was. It was hard to believe the night they'd waited for had arrived. More than anything Jill wanted to get it over with.

At eleven o'clock she went up to her bedroom. There weren't any rules about Friday night bedtimes, but she felt that she just couldn't sit still another minute.

Once in her bedroom, Jill decided there was no need to undress for bed. She would just have to dress again in order to meet David and Bernard at the Capitol at midnight.

She fiddled around with things in her room and re-arranged her collection of miniature animals. Long ago she started collecting elephants, and then she had bought a handmade ceramic toad at the church bazaar. Her mother called her collection a menagerie—a word Bernard would like.

Fingering the fat little warty toad, she remembered distinctly the lady who made it saying this was a toad, not a frog. She pointed out how she'd been careful to mold the raised glands above the exposed eardrum, as this distinguishes toads from frogs. And, the frog's skin is moist and smooth while the toad's is rough.

All of a sudden, Jill felt a strange prickling sensation at the back of her neck. Why, of all the animals on her shelf, had she singled out this one to ponder over—tonight of all nights! What had she read in the ghost story book? That toads were witches' companions? Rod's words came back to her: "Do you cut off toads' heads and put them in your cauldron?"

With a shudder, Jill replaced the little brownish toad and went to her closet. From the top shelf she took down her small treasure box. For the past two nights she had not allowed herself to look at the lock of hair. She had begun feeling so eerie just thinking of it, she hadn't dared take it out of its hiding place.

As she slowly opened the box, she had the strangest feeling that the hair may not even be there. But it was . . . and she breathed a sigh of relief. It was just where she had placed it, right on top of the ticket stub from a Carolina ball game.

Ever so carefully she picked it up. A sudden sweet smell—like the sweet shrub tree at her grandmother's—engulfed her. How peculiar! She brought the hair up to her nose. The fragrance didn't seem to come from the lock, and yet there had been no such smell in the room until she opened the box. Quickly she looked at the other contents, tumbling them with her free hand. There was absolutely nothing else that could have put out that fragrance. That was odd.

For the hundredth time she looked at the clock. And then she sat on the edge of her bed and began to count slowly to sixty, measuring her counting against the clock to see if it really equalled a minute.

By the time she had tired of this, the house was quiet. Jill tiptoed down the hall and to the head of the stairs. All the lights were out. In a strange house, she would not have been able to navigate in the dimness, but she hoped her familiarity would prevent her from bumping into furniture.

She slipped softly back to her room, watched the second hand of her clock go around several more times, and turned off her light.

Clutching the lock of hair, she took a deep breath and began her ghostly march downstairs.

IX.

Entering

Black clouds snaked across the moon as Jill eased the back door shut and stepped out into the damp night. The thin light from the street lamp ridged the hedges in darkness.

She stopped abruptly and stood still. Was there something on the other side of the hedge? Was the ghost watching her? Did he know she had the lock of hair?

Darn David! He could have met me at the hedge and we could have gone to the Capitol together, she thought anxiously. But, no, Bernard had felt it would be better if they went to the Byrnes statue separately—everything had to be done *nonchalantly*.

Jill's heart dropped into the pit of her stomach as she held her breath and made a quick plunge through the dew-covered shrubbery. Something moved beneath her feet throwing her off-balance and sending her sprawling headlong into the moist weeds.

She was about to scream out when she saw Beelzebub dart into the light and then streak in the opposite direction, his tail as taut as the brush her mother used to clean Bobby's baby bottles.

Causing her even more panic, Jill realized that the fall had jolted the lock of hair from her clutched hand. On her hands and knees, she groped frantically over the damp ground. It had to be here! Unless . . . unless Bee had taken it! . . . But, he wouldn't have taken it. He was too frightened of it. That was what sent him into these crazy rages!

Just then Jill's hand touched something that felt like the faded ribbon. She grabbed it and held it up to the street lamp's faint yellow light. "Thank heavens," she breathed. "David and Bernard would have killed me!"

Not until she got to her feet and began hurrying toward the street did Jill feel the sharp pain in her knee. With her free hand she reached down. Her jeans had been torn and her knee was badly scraped—she could tell that. Nevertheless, she'd have to hurry.

Just as she was about to step out into the street, she saw a police car cruising down Sumter, moving very slowly. Had someone called them? Had David or Bernard been seen? Her stomach twisted uneasily as she darted behind a tree. She'd be picked up in no time flat at this hour of the night if she were spotted.

A sudden breeze scurried in little whirls, giving motion to the trees and sending down a brittle branch in her path. Was this a warning? If the wind was up, tonight may not do at all. Bernard said *they* liked still nights. At least there was a moon, even if odd-shaped clouds kept blocking it. She had teased Bernard about witches on broomsticks, but now she dared not look up at the sky. Weren't witches always silhouetted against a cold moon?

Jill swallowed, but there was no moisture in her throat. Never had she been out alone at this hour.

So tense her muscles ached, she picked up her pace and headed toward their meeting place. As she hurried, a small thought buried in the recesses of her mind became apparent: when she had picked up the fallen lock of hair, it felt exactly like the damp grass. Until she'd seen the ribbon, she hadn't been sure it was really the lock of hair. Where had she heard a story about a fisherman who found a dead body floating and at first believed the hair to be mossy weeds?

Jill was breathing hard. Her heart floundered madly in her chest as she searched the corner grounds for a sign of the boys.

She was upon them before she realized they were crouching in the shrubbery. She jumped as David's voice croaked, "Where have you been? Did you bring the hair?"

"Yes," she whispered back. As she crouched down she thought, *if only you knew!*

For a moment the three of them huddled there. Then David's voice croaked again as he said, "We've got to wait for the security guard to go around again. We could have gone a while ago if you'd been here."

Somewhere in the distance a dog howled. Jill wondered whether animals could sense the presence of the supernatural?

Just then she noticed that Bernard had something under his arm. "What's that?" she asked, surprised at the strangeness of her own voice.

"A book, a bell, and a candle—for the ritual." His

face was solemn under light made dimmer by the gathering mist.

"What about the weather?" Jill asked in a low voice.

"I'm somewhat skeptical." Bernard tried to whisper, but his voice cracked and jerked. "An overcast sky isn't good at all. But it may rain, and storms and hard rains are great."

Great? As far as Jill was concerned, that was all they needed. Her knee was smarting terribly, but there was no need to mention it. It would only make the boys angry with her if she couldn't keep up. David would probably even say she was clumsy for falling. Besides, she hadn't known they were going to have to go through a long rigmarole in this exorcising bit. Why couldn't they just leave the hair for the ghost if that was what he wanted and get out?

"Jill, are you sure you unlocked the window?" asked David in a harsh voice.

"I already told you this afternoon that I did. It didn't look nailed down, but I don't think it had been raised in a long, long time."

"Maybe one of us oughta go ahead and try it," he said.

"I think we oughta stay together," said Jill.

"Yes," agreed Bernard. "If we get the window up, we'll need to get inside in a hurry. We can't take a chance on leaving the window open."

"I guess you're right," replied David in a hushed voice.

Jill could hear a car racing its motor at a traffic light on the lower side of the Capitol, but there was almost no traffic on Gervais Street. She wondered if it was always this quiet at midnight.

94

"There he comes now," David whispered, and they all eased up. "Stay low," he added, "and wait for my signal."

They stood stock-still and waited in absolute silence. In a flash David put out his arm to halt them. "Listen!" he said.

The wind had increased and now whirled around their feet and flapped the pant legs of their jeans. It actually made a swishing sound, almost like water, as it began to rise up and up. Then it gave a moan high in the trees above their heads.

"Gol—ly!" whispered David.

Jill took a shivery breath and looked up. The wind was pushing misshapen, inky clouds across the moon. She looked at Bernard and David. Their skin was covered with dark shadows that resembled moon spots. The splotches shifted over their faces and clothing, giving them an eerie, ghostly appearance. With a start, Jill realized she must appear that way to them too.

"Okay," whispered David. "Stay on the grass. It'll muffle our footsteps."

Fear prodded Jill's legs as she ran through the foggy mist. The trees and statues were like spectral figures lurking beneath the glow of the tall lamps as the three ghost hunters raced across the Capitol grounds toward their destination, the window.

In moments they were straining, pushing for all they were worth, to raise the window.

"Wait," said David breathlessly. "One—two—three —go!"

The screech of the window put them in a frenzy. They scrambled in, pushing and pulling each other and falling in a thud on the floor. Their eyes soon adjusted to the semi-darkness. The only light was that coming in through the window from the lamps outside, and it flickered about the room as the wind shifted the tree branches.

Suddenly something small and black shot past them.

"What was that?" croaked David.

"Oh, my soul!" exclaimed Jill. "I think it was Beelzebub. He hasn't been home in three days."

"He acted wild," Bernard said.

"It's . . . it's this hair." Jill was still careful to keep her voice low. "I didn't tell you before, but it . . . it affects him."

"Then why did he follow us?" asked David in a thin voice, and Jill realized they were still crouching in a huddle below the window.

But there was no time to answer. Bernard pulled himself up and began tugging at the window with his free hand. Just as they pulled it shut, Jill noticed a circle of yellow light moving over the opposite wall.

"Th—there's a guard outside with a flashlight," she stammered. "He heard us."

Jill was sure there was no marrow in her bones as the three of them bent low and crept toward the exit to the lower lobby. They had to get out of this room before someone came to search it! The outside security guard was probably contacting a guard on the inside on his walkie-talkie right now.

Luck was with them. The door was unlocked. David stuck his head out, peered around, and waited. Then he motioned for them to follow. They tiptoed frantically across the lobby and were about to dash up the steps when the muffled voice on the walkie-talkie reached their ears.

97

David made a beeline for the tall Visitors' Desk. The others followed and they crouched low behind it.

They strained to catch sounds and heard the firm heavy steps of the guard as he headed toward the lobby. Then he began to whistle. Jill thought of the old saying "a whistle in the house invites the Devil in."

Breathing fast, they all listened. The whistle came nearer . . . and stopped. They heard the sound of shuffling feet, then a doorknob clicked.

"2-40 to 2-16. There's no one here. 2-40 clear."

"Leave the lights on in there," was the response that came back through the speaker.

"Don't tell me you're starting this ghost bit too, Buster?"

Silence. . . .

Then Jill heard what sounded like a scuffle—or, *maybe*, she thought, *it's just the blood throbbing in my arteries.*

Then there was a rush of footsteps and a bloodcurdling scream that sounded half animal, half human.

"Dad blame!"

"What's going on in there?" The voice of the outside guard came through loud and clear.

"A consarned cat—*a black one at that!*"

"If he hurts Bee—" Jill started up, but David pulled her back down.

"Don't worry," he whispered. "He can't catch him."

They could tell both guards were in the lobby now.

"How'd that cat get in here?"

"Beats me."

The guards' footsteps seemed to be moving away.

"Come on," said David. "Let's make a dash for the stairs."

Their sneakers moved almost soundlessly across the lobby and up the broad steps of the other side. Jill almost slipped in her haste. Her heart was beating so fast, she thought surely it would crash through her ribs.

The faint slanting light in the rotunda cast inky shadows over the palmetto trees and the statue of John C. Calhoun. The red carpet appeared black.

Bernard led the way up another flight of stairs to the railed balcony. Hypnotically, Jill followed, still clutching the lock of hair.

In front of her she saw the dark shadows of David and Bernard as they fumbled with a key at the locked entrance to the dome.

"Watch for them," David spoke softly to her. "If you see anyone, we'll get behind that desk. But don't get in front of that window, or they can see you."

Jill turned slightly to see the oval window behind her. It looked down on Main Street. The lights from there shimmered up at her in a ghostly haze. David and Bernard stooped at her feet, where they worked furiously with the keys David had brought. Jill could tell David was trying each one and frantically discarding it. Finally he said dejectedly, "They won't open it." He was about to get up when Bernard pulled something from the packet he'd been clutching under his arm. "Here," he said, "try this, but hold the clapper."

Jill saw David take the small bell from Bernard, grab the clapper so it wouldn't ring and turn the knife-like handle toward the lock. Inserting it in the crack between the door and the facing, he began to work it upward toward the lock.

The door creaked open.

"It'll probably lock back." Jill barely recognized her

own voice.

"That's good," whispered David. "Then they won't know we're up here."

"Don't forget," cautioned Jill as they moved into a small, dark, closet-like room, "the guard told us it was bugged."

"Only if it's turned on from the main desk," said David. "I expect they're still chasing Beelzebub."

"If they hurt him—"

"Don't worry, Jill," Bernard whispered over his shoulder. "Cats have nine lives."

Already he was mounting the dark ladder steps leading to the dome.

X.

Exorcism

Cautiously they climbed the wooden ladder. Small whirlwinds seemed to be coming up from the darkness below. It was as if air gathered in little puffs and pushed at Jill's legs and then at her head. For a moment she thought she would have that *floating* feeling again, and then she placed her foot on solid brick.

A dry, dusty smell greeted them as they stepped off the ladder and began groping along the boarded walk that turned and twisted before it led to more steps. These were not steep like the ladder, but they were open underneath. Jill looked down and gasped. Below them gaped a black pit.

Stooping beneath large venting ducts that glistened in the faint light, they inched their way toward the dome. The nooks and crannies of the drafty rooms stretched dark and mysterious in the gloomy half-light.

A ghost story Jill had once heard darted through her

mind. *One step—two steps—three steps. . . . Were they with each step coming closer to a vampire whose clutches they could never escape?*

High empty laughter wafted up to them and hung in the open rafters. They stopped dead in their tracks.

"That's probably the guards laughing because they let a cat scare them," whispered David.

"It didn't sound to me like it came from down there," Jill whispered back.

"That's because it reverberated," explained Bernard, still making every effort to keep his voice low.

"How much farther?" asked Jill.

"It must be just around here," said Bernard, leading the way along the railed boardwalk and through another doorway and an even larger room.

Jill couldn't believe her eyes. There before them— just an arm's length from the walkway—was the dome, like a gigantic cup turned upside down. For some reason it was draped with a dark cloth-like material that made it even more foreboding in the dim red light. Jill knew that from the outside the whole dome appeared lighted, but inside there was only a faint reddish hue.

For a moment Jill just stood there, holding onto the rail with one hand and clutching the lock of hair in the other. Suddenly, the boardwalk became a witch's walk and the black pit her cauldron.

A creak of boards and a peculiar smell made Jill think of graveyards. She stood rooted to that one spot with the lock of hair grasped in her damp palm.

Something fluttered near her head and she ducked. In the faint light she saw the silhouette of a candlefly. It dashed itself against one of the many oval-shaped upper windows on the outside walls of the room supporting the dome.

David, who was sitting to Jill's right, spun around. "L—look!" he said.

Two small round balls of light were suspended in the darkness. But Jill had seen those *eyes* too many nights to be frightened. "It's only Bee," she said. "But how did he get up here?" She leaned over and called to him softly.

Beelzebub responded by leaping somewhere into the blackness beneath them.

A gust of wind swept wildly around their legs. Like a small whirlwind it lifted up the great canvas covering the dome and straightened it out like a flying carpet. In the next moment the coarse cloth had cupped itself down again over the tremendous dome. Before they could grasp what had happened, there was a raking screech and something exploded. Jill gasped.

"What broke?" asked David.

"It sounded like light bulbs," answered Bernard. "At any rate, the electricity is off." He added hurriedly, "Come on. Stoop down. I'm going to light the candle."

"Do you have to?" asked Jill, mindful of her scraped knee as she crouched down.

"It'll scare the evil spirits away," he said. His face appeared thin and grotesque as he bent over to light the black candle he had brought for the ceremony. The faint flicker of the tiny flame created even deeper shadows around them. Bernard reached his hand toward Jill. "Let me have the lock of hair."

Very carefully he positioned the hair at the base of the candle. "Now," Bernard said in a solemn high-pitched voice, "look at the flame and try to think of absolutely nothing."

103

Jill tried hard to push every thought from her mind, but she couldn't keep herself from thinking of the trouble they could get into for lighting a match in the dome.

As she watched, the light seemed to leave the candle and float about in space, waver, and come back.

"All right," said Bernard, his voice still pitched high, "we don't have any way of knowing in what form the spirit will manifest itself. It may even be transparent." Then he drew a long shaky breath and began.

At first what he said was in a low chant. Jill strained to hear. Mostly it sounded like syllables but not words. Then he paused and she heard him say in a sing-song voice, "Oh, spirit, we would like to help you." He paused. "If you will let us help you, rap once."

His measured words echoed in the dome and fell back upon them.

Silence. . . . Then, a grinding sound.

Jill felt clammy cold from head to foot.

"*Bump!*"

They all grew rigid as if an electric shock had gone through their bodies. Was that the poltergeist answering? The bump had been muffled like a hammer wrapped in a towel hitting a wooden object—but it had been quite distinct.

"Are you there?" asked Bernard in a strange hollow voice.

"*Bump!*"

"Does one bump mean yes?"

"*Bump!*"

"Two bumps mean no?"

"*Bump! Bump!*"

"Are you a male poltergeist?"

"*Bump!*"

There was a raking screech.

"Let me ask him something," croaked Jill.

"All right," said Bernard, "but hurry. We don't know how long we can keep him called up."

"Are you the kind of gh—, I mean spirit, that throws things?" she asked in a breathless voice.

"*Bump!*"

Jill's fear became edged with anger. If he was that kind, then she thought they should forget about trying to help him.

David took a deep breath and asked, "Did you lose a lock of hair?"

Abruptly the air became heavier and harder to breath. An earsplitting clap of thunder jolted them. It was as if the world they were in had broken loose from its ordered place and they were being flung about in chaos.

Lightning streaked across the dome, briefly illuminating their pale faces. And then pitch darkness. Even the faint flicker from the candle had been snuffed.

Jill felt herself go limp.

Then something, which sounded like hundreds of tiny rocks, began to beat violently against the roof of the dome.

So he is the rock throwing type, Jill thought. Why had they even tried to be nice to him?

Bernard's voice lifted above the thunderous beat. "That's hail," he said. "There's a thunderstorm."

Now we're really sunk, thought Jill, as they sat engulfed in pitch blackness relieved only by flashes of lightning. Even if they got out of the dome alive, they'd never get out of the Capitol Building without being

106

caught. The downpour had surely chased all the guards inside, and she, David, and Bernard could never get by all of them.

For a while the three seemed frozen into position. Then Jill watched as Bernard struck a match across the small matchbook cover, only to have it go out before he could relight the candle. Again and again he tried, cupping his hands to protect the small glow from the mysterious puffs of wind that circled them.

Finally he said, "That's all. I don't have any more matches."

"Gosh," said David, "We should've brought a flashlight."

Jill thought she had been afraid before, but no feelings she'd ever had could match hers at this moment. What would they see before them when the lights came on again? Would some black shapeless image be writhing in the shadows? Or would a goblin with fiery eyes and a sickly green grin be dangling over them?

Jill was numb with fear. She momentarily wished her parents would realize she had disappeared and come looking for her. Why had the three of them been foolish enough to do this stupid thing anyway? Judging by David's and Bernard's faces when they were revealed in the flashes of light, Jill saw that they felt the same way.

Again the sickeningly sweet smell engulfed Jill. Her head swam as they crouched like carved figures, waiting . . . waiting. . . .

Now and then a rumble broke the eerie silence. Was it thunder or something supernatural moving through the sky? And where was Beelzebub? Occasionally Bernard called out in a hollow voice, "Oh, spirit, are you still there?" But there was never an answer—only the dying thunder.

Finally David spoke. "I think it's stopped raining," he said. "We might as well go."

"How can we," Jill heard herself ask, "in this pitch blackness?"

"She's right," said Bernard. "The rail doesn't go all the way."

Jill shuddered.

After what seemed an eternity, the lights came on again. Never did Jill think she would be so glad to see the uncanny red glow of the dome. Even the distorted faces of David and Bernard were a welcomed sight.

Then Jill gasped. *"The hair! It's gone!"*

"Maybe it fell," said David, running his hands over the planks near him.

Still in squatting positions, Jill and David felt along the boardwalk immediately around them.

"It couldn't have fallen," said Bernard. "It was in the center of the boardwalk by the candle."

"Maybe Beelzebub took it," said David.

"Oh, no, he wouldn't have touched it," said Jill.

"Then . . . ." David hesitated.

"The spirit took it," Bernard finished up for him.

"Do you really think so?" asked Jill. "But—" Then her hand, still flattened and searching the board for the lock of hair, touched something. Was it a rock? None of the *rocks* that were thrown sounded like they'd been in the room with them, but as if they had pelted some outside surface.

"Look!" she said, holding the flat round object up in the dimness.

"Here," said Bernard, "let me see. . . . Why, it's a

button!"

"A button?" asked David.

"Yes," Bernard answered. "The poltergeist must have left it as a sign that he took the hair."

"Really?" asked Jill, not as willing as Bernard to accept all these supernatural doings.

"Don't you see?" Bernard's voice actually sounded excited. "If the button came from an old Civil War uniform as I expect it did, then that would be final proof that he was the person in the Capitol Aunt Becky told us about." He returned the button to Jill and began to gather up the bell, book, and candle.

"It . . . it smells moldy," she said.

"Come on," said David, getting to his feet. "Let's get out of here."

At that moment, the dome became flooded with bright light. A rush of human footsteps told them they were trapped. There was nowhere to hide on the plank boardwalk that encircled the dome.

From somewhere below a man's voice shouted, "Follow me and keep me covered!"

The three were still frozen in place and wild-eyed when the first guard burst through the open doorway, gun in hand.

The anxious expression on his face softened when he saw what confronted him. "Hey, Smitty," he called as he lowered his gun, "hurry on up here; we got us three kids."

The events of the next few minutes melted in utter confusion. The second guard looked angry and demanded to know what in tarnation they were doing in the Capitol at this time of night and, specifically, why there were in the dome.

Jill and David both looked at Bernard, who was still blinking against the sudden light. Bernard took his time gathering his thoughts. As he spoke, they watched the guards trying to comprehend Bernard's explanation.

"You mean you've rid the Capitol of its ghost?" the first guard asked, casting a knowing yet suspicious look at his companion.

Then they marched them over the treacherous walks and down the steps to the main desk in the lower lobby, where no amount of pleading would keep the guards from calling their parents and the chief security guard. When Bernard told them he didn't have a phone, Jill thought they looked as if they didn't believe him. And when he said his parents probably weren't at home anyway, they said they'd check it out.

The chief guard was so gruff when he came in, Jill wondered if he realized that what they had done was for his own good. Now he wouldn't have to worry about the night guards quitting because of the scraping and bumping noises. Jill was glad when Bernard proceeded quite long-windedly to tell him so.

The next thing Jill knew, the chief guard was on his desk phone. "Bill," he said, "I think you oughta come on down to the State House. I've got a real hot story for you."

Before Jill knew what was happening, people were pouring into the Capitol. Her mom and dad showed up first, then David's grandmother and a newspaper reporter.

With a frown, which clearly indicated his dissatisfaction, Jill's dad came right up to her and asked her "the meaning of this." David's grandmother, with a flushed face, requested the same of the tight-faced se-

110

curity guard.

Of all the adults, only the reporter seemed poised. He edged up behind them and began asking questions. How had they found out about the ghost? he wanted to know. David's answer—"from a news clipping"—had brought a smile. How had they determined he was a poltergeist? Why had they become interested in this? Where had they gotten their knowledge? Had they been scared? And on and on. . . .

When the interview came to a lull, Jill's father said, "Of course we can't keep you from printing this in the paper, but you won't give their names? They *are* under sixteen."

The reporter, who had been taking hurried notes, assured them no names would be printed. On his way out, he leaned over the desk and whispered something to the chief guard, and for the first time the scowling lines of the security officer's face broke into a broad grin.

The guard they called Smitty stood by Bernard, waiting to escort him to Claire Towers. As the group broke up and everyone prepared to leave, Smitty spoke to their parents. "Don't be too hard on them," he said. "At least our night passed more quickly than usual."

When Jill woke up at noon the next day, she knew even before she looked down that the spot of warmth in the bend of her legs was Beelzebub. Jill leaned down and kissed his head. "You know, Bee, that tortured spirit really owes his peace to you. If you hadn't sidetracked the guards, we'd never have gotten into the dome." Beelzebub purred, and somehow Jill felt he had known that all along.

Brilliant sunshine spilled through the tall bedroom

window. At that moment the events of last night seemed no more than a wild, crazy dream.

Jill scrambled out of bed and picked up the button from her dresser. She'd realized last night after she got home that the button did indeed, as Bernard had said, come from an old army uniform—maybe the very one the hair had fallen from. But so much had happened and Jill was so tired and sleepy she had just kept quiet about the button and her sore knee. She knew one thing for sure: Mrs. Smith would be interested in knowing about this button.

There were still many unanswered questions—and much that Jill would never understand. But, she wondered, how had Beelzebub gotten into the dome? And why had Bernard brought the bell? Maybe she would ask him that.

As she slipped into her clothes, she was glad she'd had the encounter with her parents last night. At least she didn't have that to face this morning.

She was even more relieved when Michael told her that Mom had gone to the garden with Dad. In the next breath, he wanted to know about the ghost.

"Who told you?" she asked, realizing that she would now have to put up with the teasing of her brothers—especially Rod.

"Dad read it to us at the breakfast table this morning."

With that, Jill ran to the dining room. There she found *The State* newspaper folded so the article on the lower front page was showing. As fast as she could Jill read the piece.

Has the Ghost in the Capitol
Been Exorcised?

Three youngsters claim to have soothed the restless spirit believed by many to have haunted the South Carolina State Capitol for decades.

The ritual, complete with bell, book, and candle, was performed in the early morning hours after the trio gained entry through a ground-floor window.

C. R. Hall, chief security guard, made no charges against the two boys and one girl but turned them over to the custody of their parents.

"There is," he said, "one mystery that as yet has not been solved. Every other light bulb in the dome was shattered during the 'exorcism.' It would have been impossible for the kids to have done that damage." Laughing nervously, he continued, "Sure they'll be expensive to replace, but in exchange for peaceful nights, it will be worth it."

Sharply reprimanded by their parents for their nocturnal venture, the youngsters will undoubtedly involve themselves in projects of a different nature in the future.

Have they really rid the Capitol of its ghost? Only time will tell.

"Thank heavens they didn't say who we were," Jill sighed with relief, "or we'd never hear the last of it at school."

More than anything at this moment she wanted to see Aunt Becky. Too restless to think of eating, she dashed out the door and through the hedge to David's house. Places that had appeared so ghostly the night before were now warm and familiar. The hard rain had washed all the trees and shrubs, and the air smelled fresh and clean. Jill felt as far from witches and magic as anyone could get, and that was exactly the way she wanted it.

David's grandmother was hanging her dish towels on the back porch to dry. "Hello, Jill," she said. "I think we're all feeling better this morning, but I do hope you and David have learned a lesson."

"Oh, yes, ma'am," she replied, "you don't have to worry about that."

"I'm not so sure," she mused, as they entered the kitchen, "that the new boy with all that supernatural hogwash is not a bad influence on you two."

"Oh, no, ma'am," Jill said hurriedly. "Bernard's all right." As Jill heard herself say it, she realized that sometime during their horrifying experience, she had come to accept Bernard. In fact, she had never thought they would find a replacement for Steve. But as far as she was concerned, they had. She knew they would always miss Steve, but Bernard was okay.

"Go on into Aunt Becky's room," his grandmother said. "David's in there, and for a change, *he's* telling the stories." She gave Jill a friendly pat on the shoulder.

When Jill walked into the room she noticed that Aunt Becky's eyebrows were raised in the shape of a perfect "housetop" on her forehead.

It appeared that Aunt Becky wasn't one bit put out with them over the exorcising affair.

"Well, Jill," she said, patting *The State* in her lap with a devilish smile on her face, "we won't have to look any farther for David's current event next week, will we?"

"Oh, no, you don't," David said. "I'm through with ghosts . . . *forever*."

David told Jill he had already been to Bernard's. The Thornburgs had returned home by the time the officer arrived with Bernard, but they weren't very upset when they found out why he was away. "But," David continued, "they said he should have told the landlord where he was going." Jill giggled aloud at that.

114

Mr. Thornburg, David told her, had even asked Bernard to write it all down for the record.

"Oh, no!" screamed Jill. But Aunt Becky assured her she wanted to see a copy of it.

That evening when the Johnston family gathered for dinner, Jill was more surprised than ever. Rod didn't tease her as she had expected. Instead, he kept asking questions about the reaction of the poltergeist. "Next time," he said seriously, "I want to be in on it."

But before Jill had time to respond, her mother assured him there wouldn't be a next time.

The End

About the author:

IDELLA BODIE was born in Ridge Spring, South Carolina. She received her degree in English from Columbia College and taught high school English and creative writing for thirty-one years. She has been writing books for young readers since 1971.

Mrs. Bodie lives in Aiken with her husband Jim. In her spare time, she enjoys reading, gardening, and traveling.

About the illustrator:

GAY HAFF KOVACH is a freelance illustrator and graphic artist. An honors graduate of the Ringling School of Art and Design, Ms. Kovach has illustrated several children's books and her artwork has appeared on book and magazine covers, posters, and billboards. She owns and operates a portrait and greeting card business called Sweet Art in Gaston, South Carolina.

She has illustrated three of Mrs. Bodie's other books: *Whopper, The Mystery of Edisto Island,* and *Trouble at Star Fort.* She also provided the cover for *Spunky Revolutionary War Heroine.*